COBRA

E. P. DUTTON & CO., INC. NEW YORK • 1975

COBRA

SEVERO SARDUY

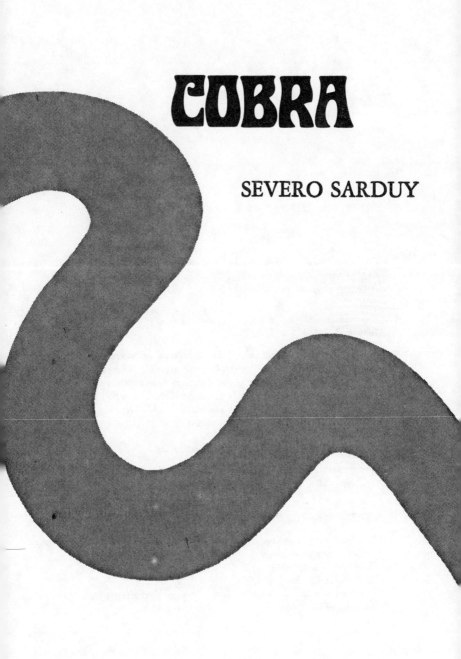

First Edition

10 9 8 7 6 5 4 3 2 1

Library of Congress Cataloging in Publication Data

Sarduy, Severo.
  Cobra.

  I. Title.
PZ4.S2482Co [PQ7390.S28]   863   74–7041

Published simultaneously in Canada by Clarke, Irwin & Company Limited,
Toronto and Vancouver
ISBN: 0-525-08237-9
Designed by The Etheredges
Assistance for the translation of this volume was given by the Center for
Inter-American Relations.

CONTENTS

COBRA II

PREFACE

Cobra represents, in many ways, the culmination of the New Latin American Novel. Perhaps, to suggest an even more apocalyptical vision, it represents a turning point in the course of the novel form. The Novel as a genre officially introduced itself in the sixteenth century as a picaresque account, as the pseudo-autobiographical narration of a rogue's adventures in a "modern" era that was, like all others but maybe more so, hallucinatory. *Cobra* also tells the particular and universal adventures of a versatile rogue but this time the rogue is the text itself. Sarduy weaves in "astounding" details on astronomical life beyond earth's bounds as well as fictitious reports on the frivolities of the West and on the rituals of the inscrutable East. The hallucinatory universe in which these adventures take place is, again, the text: In the sense that *Cobra* narrates and comments on its own "story," its own "life," it is the Novel come full circle, the snake biting its tail.

The relationship between Part I and Part II of *Cobra,* like the interrelationship of all the segments of the novel, is one of reflection, of narrative threads which interweave, of voices which parody—in the sense of commenting, of reflecting on and upon—each other.

Part I tells the tale of a fastidious transvestite, Cobra, whose great desire or passion is to transform his/her body. Hopefully, (s)he will find compensation for her efforts and suffering in her starring role as Queen in the Lyrical Theater of Dolls. This metamorphic ritual, whose correspondence cannot be found in Western culture, is comparable only to the rigorous dedication with which actors in the religious theaters of India strive to convert themselves into their masquerades, for days on end.

The Madam, a kind of jack(?)-of-all-trades, and Pup, a witty dwarf (and Cobra's tiny double), form with Cobra a rather dubious Trinity. This parodic configuration is already present in Sarduy's previous novel, *De donde son los cantantes* (1967) (*From Cuba with a Song,* in *Triple Cross,* Dutton, 1971). The Madam and Pup assist and accompany Cobra in her metamorphoses, as they themselves change with her, as, again, the text changes shape, fragments, re-forms, an incessantly mutating organism under a high-power microscope.

In Part II, Cobra is initiated into what is perhaps a band of leather boys who have taken on fetish names and whose cardboard ceremonies seem like a dream . . . or into a sect of Tibetan lamas who struggle, far from their "pristine sources," to revive their rituals. This adventure is staged in the suburbs of Paris, or in Chinese landscapes. The Search here, rather than toward identity, is toward eroticism, an absence. The last chapter, the Indian Journal, traces a journey and the counterplay between statement and commentary, East and West, which the whole novel voices.

This presentation of the basic "plot" offers one reading of *Cobra*. However, it soon becomes obvious, as I suggested before, that the Orient, like the theater world of Cobra the actress in Part I, is another deforming mirror. Unlike Herman Hesse, Sarduy does not pretend to deal with a transcendental India but rather with what is visible, its surface. In this sense, *Cobra* can be seen not only as a commentary on mysticism "made easy," but also, in all its jubilant Pop aspects, as a glorification of camp phenomena—one thinks of movies like *Cobra Woman* and *Cult of the Cobra*, although *Cobra* is not to be regarded as a sequel to these.

The East is a transvestite of the West in the western imagination of Severo Sarduy. In an interview with E. Rodríguez Monegal, Sarduy has pointed out that:

> . . . *we're not talking about a transcendental, metaphysical or profound India, but on the contrary, about an exaltation of the surface and I would say costume jewelry India. I believe . . . that the only decoding Westerners can do, that the only unneurotic reading that is possible from our logocentric point of view, is that which India's surface offers. The rest is Christianizing translation, syncretism, real superficiality.*

Like the theater, the East is an emblem of parody, again in the sense of commentary, of apotheosis as well as of mockery. A parodical text—that is, a text that comments on itself—*Cobra* is therefore emblematic of textual dimensions, or negatively emblematic of the unreality of the text *outside* of its own surface. Its identity, its meaning, can be found in its surface which is its only "reality." Words serve to approach meaning, but perhaps meaning is only that endless approach. Celebrations of themselves (like eroticism), words fulfill that other aspect of parody which is apotheosis, carnival, humor.

In his two previous novels, *Gestos* (Gestures, 1963) and *From Cuba with a Song,* both set, primarily, in a timely and timeless Cuba, and also in his book of essays, *Escrito sobre un cuerpo* (Written on a Body, 1969), Sarduy constantly reveals, through an emblematic writing, that in the written text, words can only be metaphors. Now, in *Cobra,* a more obviously utopic novel that is set everywhere and nowhere, he is again suggesting that history is fiction, life is theater, a place is a textual painting.

If this is the case, then another level of reading would be even more fruitful than the lineal one.

The key to this other level can be found in the words themselves, or more concretely, in the title. COBRA alludes to the COBRA school of painting,* as well as to the verb *cobrar,* meaning "to collect payment." It also suggests *barroco* (baroque) and Córdoba, remnant of the Arabian empire in the south of Spain. Cobra, the snake, the actress, the verb, the symbol of a pictorial school, is the novel. Or, since both ends of the sacred serpent meet in an ellipse—the ellipse is a more complex and ambiguous form than the circle because it has two centers, one visible, one absent—it can be said that this novel is an infinite play (within its finite nature) of transformations and repetitions branching from the vocable "cobra" as it winds its way along its slippery, rootless route.

It is this playful route, or reading, which the translation, perhaps equally devious, attempts to follow. Naturally, translators must try to capture the exact meanings of words, but it soon becomes evident that the only fidelity possible in this poetic text is a fidelity to the system of relationships native to the text. I refer not only to the relationships between words and between

* An anagram formed from the three cities—COpenhagen, BRussels, Amsterdam—where the artists work.

levels of writing which can be recognized in the apparent transformations and repetitions, visible in the "basic" plot itself, but
also to the relationship between proteic *Cobra* and her alert
reader. If *Cobra* is a playful series of transmutations, then the
translation of *Cobra* is one more metamorphosis in this spiral-
ing series of "events."

I would like to express my thanks to those who came to my
assistance in the process of this translation, especially Professor
Roberto González Echevarría of Cornell University and Enrico
Santi at Yale University.

SUZANNE JILL LEVINE

COBRA I

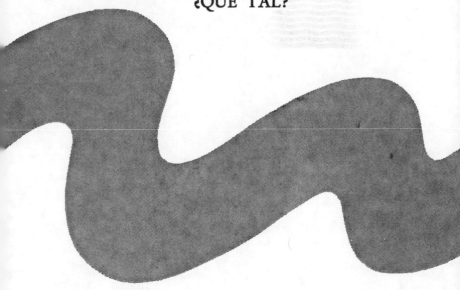

LYRICAL THEATER OF DOLLS

I

She'd set them in molds at daybreak, apply salt compresses, chastise them with successive baths of hot and cold water. She forced them with gags; she submitted them to crude mechanics. She manufactured wire armors, to put them in, shortening and twisting the threads again and again with pliers; after smearing them with gum arabic she bound them with strips of cloth: they were mummies, children of Florentine medallions.

She attempted scrapings.

Resorted to magic.

Fell into orthopedic determinism.

COBRA. "My God"—on the record player Sonny Rollins, of course—"why did you bring me into the world if it wasn't to be absolutely divine?"—she moaned naked on an alpaca rug, among fans and Calder mobiles. "What good is it to be queen of the Lyrical Theater of Dolls, and to have the best collection of mechanical toys, if at the sight of my feet men run away and cats start climbing on them?"

She took a sip of the "pool"—that pitcher in which the Madam, to compensate for the rigors of summer and of the reducing operation, served her a raspberry ice cream soda—she smoothed her tangled glass hairs, with a metric ruler she measured the rebellious ones and again launched into the "My God, why . . . ," etc.

She began to transform at six for the midnight show; in that crying ritual one had to deserve each ornament: the false eyelashes and the crown, the pigments, which the profane could not touch, the yellow contact lenses—tiger eyes—the powders of the great white powder puffs.

Even offstage, once painted and in possession of their costumes, they obeyed the Queen, and at the mustached apparition of a Devil the servants would flee through the corridors or lock themselves in the cupboards and come out plastered with flour.

Swift, disheveled, the opposite of the pageantry onstage, the Madam would glide in Wise Monkey slippers, arranging the screens which structured that *décroché* space, that heterotopia —tavern, ritual theater and/or doll factory,[1] lyrical bawdyhouse

---

[1] Yes, because the swains would arrive in such embarrassment, that you had to push them to the place where all saints help: which the Madam did with Cosmetic's aid. The dolls would leave their cubicles in full splendor of yin, crackling with jewels like Coccinell; or on the contrary, minted like Bambi, with brown bangs and in ready-to-wears, aggressive out of pure discretion. At each show a new wave of converts would appear, another sopranoed chorus of transgressors: "Soon we'll fall into Stajanovism!"—the Madam would pro-

—whose elements only she saved from dispersion or boredom. She'd appear suddenly in the kitchen, in the orange smoke of a shrimp sauce, she'd run in and out of the dressing rooms carrying a plate of oysters, she'd prepare a syringe or lacquer a comb to twist an obstinate curl.

So the Go Between came and went, as I was saying a paragraph ago, through the corridors of that snail shell of kitchens, steam baths, and dressing rooms, crossing tip toe the dark cells where all day the mutants slept, imprisoned in machines and gauze, immobilized by threads, lascivious, smeared with white facial creams. The network of her route was concentric, her passage was spiral through the baroque setting of mosquito nets. She would watch over the hatching of her cocoons, the emerging of the silk, the winged unfolding. The Guggenheim Museum, with its centrifugal ramps, was less dizzying than this place which, muddy, reduced to a single layer, the Procuress animated with her daily roving: flattened circular castle, "labyrinth of the ear." With cotton soaked in ether she would calm the suffering, give gin tonics to the thirsty, and to those who grew impatient with the wait among compresses of burning turpentine and poultices of crushed leaves, her favorite advice: be Brechtian.

She ruled, braiding buns, reducing with ice massages, here a belly, there a knee, smoothing big hands, tuning husky rebel voices with cedar inhalations, disguising irreducible feet with a double platform and a pyramidal heel, distributing earrings and adjectives.

Cobra was her greatest accomplishment, her "rabbit-foot." Despite her feet and her shadow—cf.: chapter V—she preferred her to all the other dolls, finished or in process. From daybreak on she would select her outfits, brush her wigs, arrange on the

---

test. "We must correct the errors of natural binaryism"—she added, Benvenistian—"but *per piacere*, gentlemen, this is not like shooting fish in a barrel!"

Victorian chairs Indian cassocks with gold galloons, real and velvet cats; among the cushions she would hide toy acrobats and snake charmers which on being touched would set off a *Skater's Waltz* on a tin flute, with baritonal shrieks, so that they'd surprise Cobra at siesta time. Then she would surrender to the contemplation of the color poster which, framed between red pennants, presided over that chamber.

Dear Lady Readers:

I know that at this point you don't have the slightest doubt about the identity of the character presented so disproportionately here: of course, it's Mei Lan Fang. The octogenarian *impersonator* of the Peking Opera appeared in her characterization as a young lady—a coif of rattles on her head—receiving the bouquet of flowers, the pineapple and cigar box from the virile president of a Cuban delegation.

And when each ringlet was in its place, then the Mother would arrange rendez-vous, fulfilling the petitions of the most persistent and the high rollers, spacing out the schedules of the most solicited ones, plotting chance meetings in the cells of the least solicited. To these she'd give her best advice and reveal the weakness of each customer, to once again correct the laws of nature and rescue the always uncertain balance between supply and demand: the poor wretches knew who was foot adorer and for whom one had to do a Javanese dance in a Mata Hari costume, while having an enema.

Writing is the art of ellipsis: in vain would we point out that of all the agendas Cobra's was the most crowded. Dior was a close second with her bouquets of orchids received anonymously, Sontag for her Cartier jewels and reserved tables at Maxim's, Cadillac for the number of hours Caddy convertibles and their black chauffeurs dressed in white had waited for her and for all the other friendly presents which, before he sends his card, have already introduced a South American ranch owner.

What is really worth mentioning is that Cobra's fervent admirers rioted only to adore her close up, to remain a few moments in mute contemplation of her. A slight, pale London tea importer brought her three tambourines one night so that at their rhythm she, laden with bracelets, cymbals, torches and hoops, would prance on him, like Durga on the demon turned buffalo.

Some, coolly, would ask to kiss her hands; others, more perturbed, lick her clothes; a few, dialectic, would surrender to her, supreme derision of yang.

The Go Between would concede appointments by order of certainty in ecstasy: the contemplative and lavish would obtain her for the same night; the practitioners and close-fisted were put off for weeks and only had access to the Myth when there was no better bidder.

. . . the Mother, suddenly, would fall into a chair, fatigued. They'd fan her. Even from there she would continue directing the mise-en-scène, the traffic of movable platforms and trappings in the visible show—where Cadillac was already singing—and in the broader theater of consecutive rooms.

Writing is the art of digression. Let us speak then of a smell of hashish and of curry, of a stumbling basic English and of a tingling trinket music. This signalectic file card is the Indian costume-maker's, who three hours before curtain time would arrive with his little box of brushes, his minutely precise bottles of ink and "the wisdom"—the same turbaned one would say, in profile, displaying his only earring—"of a whole life painting the same flower, dedicating it to the same god."

And so he'd decorate the divas with his arabesques, tit by tit, since these, for being round and protuberant, were much easier to adorn than the prodigal bellies and little Boucherian buttocks, pale pink with a tendency to spread. The hoarse divinities would parade before the inventor of butterfly wings and there remain static the time to review their songs; devoted, the miniaturist would conceal *in vivo* the nudity of the frozen big-footed queens with silver orles, eye hieroglyphs, arabesques and rainbows, which came out thinner or thicker depending on the insertion and watery brew; he would disguise the shortcomings of each with black whorls and underline the charms surrounding them with white circles. On their hands he'd write, in saffron and vermilion, their cue lines, the most forgettable, and the order in which they had to recite them, and on their fingers, with tiny arrows, an outline of their first movements. They would leave the minister of external affairs, all tattooed, psychedelic, made for love from head to toe. The Madam would look them over, stick on their eyelashes and an OK label for each, and send them off with a slap on the backside and a Librium.

Writing is the art of recreating reality. Let us respect it. The Himalayan artificer did not arrive, as it was said, bejeweled and pestiferocious, but in a newly ironed and virile cream color twilled suit—on his silk tie an Eiffel tower and a naked woman lying on the *Folies Cheries* caption.

No. Writing is the art of restoring History.

The dermic silversmith fought in the court of a Maharajah, near Kashmir. He was master of holds and grimaces—which demoralize the enemy; he could, sketching a cartwheel, land on his hands and fell an aggressor with a double kick in the stomach, or whirling him around, he could thrust into the nape of his neck the very dagger with which the assailant attacks.

Waving a large madras shawl with his right hand he could hurl a javelin into the left side of a Cambodian tiger.

He believed in suggestion, in the technique of surprise and in victory being irrevocable if one succeeded in frightening the adversary with appearance; he would deform himself with patches and falsies, he'd arise before the gaping opponents with two noses or with an elephant trunk, red like a pimiento, hanging from his forehead by a spring. He learned from his daily incarnations into devil, the art of tattooing and the ventriloquist's foils, which make the rival look over his shoulder.

He had escaped the Kashmir revolution with a suitcase of jewels that he squandered among rouge-painted whores in flowered barges—the lake brothels of the north—and in fixed tournaments—they proclaimed him Invincible—against the champions from Calcutta; he had revived a wrestling school in Benares, and in Ceylon a tea concession on whose boarded floors, which overlapped in a spiral like those of a tower, obese paint-smeared matrons came to lie at nightfall, among little sacks of tea.

He was a spice importer in Colombo. He fled one night, after losing a boxing match. From the ropes that secured it to the earth, the flames reached the circus tent that sheltered the winners.

His last feat was a bluff in a Smyrna pancratium: without allowing himself intermissions he reduced to cripples six Turkish champions. So erect, so imperturbable was he when they dealt him a blow, when the giants, climbing with a jump on his belly, pulled his hair, like one who scales a cliff grabbing onto lianas, and then such was his thrust in the cat house, he celebrated his trophies by laying eunuchs and broads, that the matron—an obese Greek, mounted on heels and with a flower in his hair—won over by the philological itch and to evoke all at once his verticality in the arena and his licentious thrust, nicknamed him Eustachio.

He went over to the West then, carrying that name which was all he preserved from his gymnastic wanderings.

He concealed beneath a benign transgression—bottling coke without a license—his real infraction.

He was an ivory smuggler in the Jewish flea markets of Copenhagen, Brussels and Amsterdam; he cultivated to obsession an Oxford accent and black, shiny hair which, sticking out of a green suede hat, ended in an officially oriental, combed, straight beard.

A convex mirror and another dozen smaller ones which surrounded him multiplied his image when with a puff-cheeked servant he entered a house of white walls and white doors closed by black knockers.

Through the gothic arched windows rings of opaque glass filtered a grey and humid day. A Flemish tapestry stuck out of a Sienese trunk. Smoked herrings and silver clusters of garlic hung from the rafters. On a table there was a scale and an open bible whose initials were hypogryphs biting their tails, sirens and harpies. Reflection of a glass of wine, a transparent red line trembled over the tablecloth.

On a shelf, behind bottles of cherries in *aguardiente,* the servant hid a bag of florins.

Writing is the art of disorganizing an order and organizing a disorder.

The Madam had discovered the Indian amidst the steam of a Turkish bath, in the suburbs of Marseille. She was so amazed when, despite the prevailing vapor, she distinguished the proportions with which Vishnú had graced him—all those hieroglyphs inscribed there, used by destiny to astonish us without revealing their nature—that, without knowing why, she thought of Ganesa, the elephant god.

Let's take advantage of that steam to fade out the scene. The next one is more in focus. In it we see the fighter in full possession of his writing skill, "which veils without dressing and adorns without hiding," preparing the models of the Lyrical Theater of Dolls for the show.

With so many cocoons in flower, so many golden locks and Rubensian buttocks around him, the cipherer is in such a state that he no longer knows where to knock his head; he tries a brush stroke and gives a pinch, he finishes a flower between those edges most worthy of guarding it and then erases it with his tongue to paint another with more stamens and pistils and changing corollas. The Wide-Eyed Girls would crowd around him and with the opening of ink bottles the hustle and bustle would begin. Half-dressed, yawning and soaked, the Adam's appled fairies would await him playing anxious card games and drinking cans of beer. The jamboree that reigned in the twisting corners of the Shrine was such that the Madam no longer knew how to intimidate the ladies-in-waiting so that they would not lose their control as soon as Eustachio the Luscious appeared.

They began organizing naval battles in the bathtub, which were splashings and submerged penetrations; the "wars of flowers" ruined the Matron's art nouveau furniture.

Till one day.

The Madam appeared with a palm-leaf broom in her hand and so yellow with rage that she looked like an Asiatic steward-ess. Three playful jokers, in underclothes, had wound themselves in a red bedcover: "And Priapus rose red out of wine"—ca-roused Eustachio. Cadillac, who was going over her *bel canto* lesson in the midst of the frolic, pretended not to notice: she pressed the alarm button and continued vocalizing.

The bilious lady rushed against the spasmodic bundle as if she were putting out a fire; she launched forth with the devo-tion of one who flagellates a penitent brandishing a cat o'nine tails with ball-bearings on the tips.

She heard a *saeta*. She felt in her mouth a spongeful of vinegar. With an open hand she hit her forehead.

She went / barefoot, dragging incensories,

      / smeared with crosses of black oil,

      / in a Carmelite cassock, a yellow rope at her waist,

      / wrapped in damasks and white cloths, with a wide-brimmed hat and a staff,

/ naked and wounded, beneath a dunce cap.

She crossed   / whitewashed corridors, with wooden ships hanging from the ceiling and silver lamps in the form of ships,

/ high-domed octagonal chapels, whirlwinds of plaster angels whose walls supported shelves filled with crowns, arms and hearts of gold, opened heads revealing a wafer, small glass tubes with ashes.

In a monstrance a funeral amulet shined; in its middle circle, protected by two pieces of cut glass, surrounded by amber beads, little porous bones with filed edges were heaped—baby teeth, bird cartilage—bound by a silk hatband, lettered in black ink and gothic capitals with German names. In the sacristy the altar boys played cards. On a wooden pantry, among opaque pitchers and breads wrapped in white napkins, three silver glasses glistened.

She found herself in a town square.

The ground sloped. Over a stone arch, golden eagles, yokes, fasces of arrows, intricate knots.

She was surrounded by the entranced devotees, praying, lashing themselves, shaking wooden rattles.

SEVILLIAN MUSIC

THE MADAM—wrapped in raw silk, Torquemadesque, as in a morality play: "Half-converted!"—and a blow with her broom —"Possessed!"—she crossed herself three times, spit on the

bundle of red corduroy, beat her chest. "Poisoned leeches!"—
she sprayed the hooded trinity with *aguardiente:* she couldn't
find alcohol. "Burn, boiling bodies of worms!"

The three-cornered dunce cap: ....

When the Madam regained consciousness, she let the
ashamed and swollen threesome come out of the bundle: the
Indian, of course, Zaza and Cobra: "From this night on"—she
managed to articulate panting, addressing herself to Cadillac,
who then interrupted her trills—"you will be queen of the
Lyrical Theater of Dolls. You have shown with your example
that in art, if you want to get places, you've got to work even
if optimum conditions are not assembled. And you"—she flatly
ordered the Indian—"put on your clothes and leave. My God"
—she added sobbing—"Eustachio's tube has brought down this
house."

Which, a few days later, did not prevent the perverse fellow from communicating his nirvana to the dolls: he penetrated
floral arrangements, he contemplated them frolicking before a
Venetian mirror, spraying them with ginger he spread their legs
open on a bison rug, naked but crowned with towers of
feathers—that's where the decline of the West will lead us!—
and he lay down on the beast, face up, his hips flanked by the
horns, making them beg for it, sniffing them, prolonging the
preambles. Slow, parsimonious, with sophisticated attentions he
drew them onto himself: while the middle horn penetrated,
the side ones scraped. You couldn't tell what was making them
moan, nor when they begged for more, what more to give them.

A broken down net of wires and cables hung from the
ceiling; from the net, lamp bases, red cellophane circles, and a
broken, sparking lightbulb were suspended.

Writing is the art of patchwork. From what precedes one infers that:

if the Indian is as priapic and pleasure-prone as you have heard, he will never finish concealing with his signs the nudity of the chorus girls nor will they be able to submit impassively to the tormenting contemplation of his gifts, which is greater if you keep in mind the unbuttoning that prevails in show biz.

NOW THEN:

1) without body painting the show cannot go on; this, and even if you bribe them with increasing gratifications, is the minimal pomp which the agents of the "orgy patrol" demand; it would be worthless to resort to other coverings, nobody's interested in them;

2) without "tableaux vivants" there are no customers, nor without them can the doll factory subsist, since only when subsidized by the interested, surely, but generous, can it live;

3) without a doll factory, without a theme—*the Madam:* "Ah, because literature still needs themes . . ." I (who am in the audience): "Shut up or I'll take you out of the chapter"— this narrative cannot continue.

ERGO:

The Indian has to be as in the first version. And in fact that's how he is.

Only a moron could swallow the obviously apocryphal comic strip of the fighter who, out of the clear blue, appears in a Flemish painting and renounces his he-man strength only to fasten tight his green hat and start trafficking in florins! Come on, man!

It is true that Eustachio entertained the court of a Maharajah, but, as was to be expected, in his capacity of naked dancer and ritual choreographer; it is true that he combs "silky horse hair": he adorns it with carnations—which stay on with scotch tape—in order to dance a lively flamenco.

Nor do we lack data on his travels in the West. I will

register only one: he was identified on board "The Neutral," an establishment of rubbers and gadgets in the Red Light District of Barcelona. He would sample condoms and douche syringes; he would manufacture, in painted rubber, vomit, excrement, and worms jumping out of a cigar. The emblem of that house, likewise cacophonic, could be his life's: WONDERS OF CA-COMIC VOMIT.

If he strolls with impunity among the dolls it is because, as usual, he has placed his somatic vehicles between parentheses. Although for pleasure your edges are sufficient—Lacan explained to him one day—little does the king of bouquets enjoy his.

Order re-established in the department of pictograms, the Indian has just covered the chorus girls with silver pistils, wings of Melanesian butterflies, branches of birdlime, peacock feathers, gilded monograms, tadpoles and dragonflies, and on Cobra —who is again queen—birds of the Asiatic tropics, iridescing the phrase "Sono Assoluta" in Hindi, Bengali, Tamil, English, Kannada and Urdu.

He tests new tints on his own face, he lengthens his eyes, to be more oriental than the real thing, a ruby on his forehead, shadow on his eyelids, perfume, yes, he perfumes himself with Chanel Eustachio and he vanishes, dancing, down the corridor.

A bell.

The curtains open for the show.

Of which I shall return to tell you anon.

II

Flat anchors fixed her to the earth: Cobra's feet left something to be desired, "they were her hell." She'd set them in molds at daybreak, apply salt compresses, chastise them with successive baths of hot and cold water. She manufactured wire armors, to put them in, shortening and twisting the threads again and again with pincers; she forced them with gags; she submitted them to crude mechanics; after smearing them with gum arabic she bound them with cloth: they were mummies, children of Florentine medallions.

She attempted scrapings.

Resorted to magic.

Fell into orthopedic determinism.

At noon one day when, down at the heels, she was looking through the files of the National Library, she thought she found the solution in the *"Méthode de réduction de testes des sauvages d'Amérique selon l'a veue Messire de Champignole serviteur du roy"* (Method of Head Shrinkage among the American Savages According to the Testimony of Sire Champignole, Servant to the King). At the burlesque it was rumored that she had chartered a platoon to investigate the method *in situ,* bribing ethnologists, mortgaging her soul; it was alleged that the CIA was paying for everything, but that was only a machination of her double—Cadillac—to pull the rug from under her and replace her forever in the Lyrical Theater of Dolls.

A greenish vapor, of camphor, emanated from Cobra's dump, an arabesque which expanded into a nebulous spiral band, into a spreading snail shell of mint. Trapped in transparent flasks, boughs sprouted everywhere, wide and granular leaves, pestilent dwarf shrubs, sick flowers whose petals minute and shiny larvae gnawed at, crumpled ferns in whose folds small translucid eggs lodged, in constant multiplication. From stylized

vegetal art nouveau the cubicle had moved on to weed anarchy
—relentlessly she sought the saps, the elixir of reduction, the
juice that shrinks. In a chest of drawers and on a divan robust
artichokes opened, a white down gradually covering them; in
Lalique glasses formaldehyde preserved crushed roots and sugar-
cane knots, bagasses in which large red ants were caught.
Earthenware vessels and round lamps, upside down, protected
the germination of cotyledons from light; a mother-of-pearl
vanity case preserved seeds in alcohol, others, of tortoise shell,
snake butter, mahogany resin and nux vomica.

The bathroom supplied that laboratory. In porcelain wash
bowls, where spontaneous generation had already propagated
fly larvae, tadpoles and—Nature boasts of her miracles—even
toads, a black watercress proliferated, with thick branches and
sensitive purslane that closed its leaves at the slightest contact
and whose clusters were already covering the bidet, a white
Knoll seat—gift of Eero Saarinen—and the soap dish.

The bathtub: a field of tubular reeds, a flowery and concave Nile. Under the sink, in a Mozarabic plate pomegranates
fermented, and beans that already had shoots and spirally
striped grains, shagged like almonds, whose milk, upon souring,
carpeted the smashed polygons of a yellowing hide.

Invaded by vegetal scabs the bells of the door and the telephone filtered all signals from the outside, all calls to order.

At night one heard a continuous murmur: it was the vibra-
tory movement of the fly larvae.

—"Soon there'll be crocodiles!"—the Madam exclaimed
(she'd cover her nose with cotton soaked in *Diorissimo*) and
fled down the corridor whose rug the green scum of the jungle
was already threatening.

They accused her of witchcraft,
of weed dealing,
of breeding a wild boar in her room.

She did not care. She'd spent the day deciphering herbariums; the night boiling pits. She had initiated the Madam and the green alchemy gave them no peace: they lived amidst Latin mumbo jumbo, root squeezing and cooking branches; Cobra's feet endured the daily extract, in rigorous poultices—sure of possessing the juice that shrinks. When getting up in the morning they'd uncover them with the caution of one who digs up an Etruscan toy. According to the fissures in the plaster and the ruling astral configuration—which the Madam calculated with an ephemeride whose firmament presented mushroom signs— they would decide the next brew. Neptune in Pisces, the Madam had stated one evening, fosters shrinking, the contraction of the base, the take-off.

They were rolling easy, the astral way. But impatience is bad council. One morning screams were heard in Cobra's cell. The make-up man—an Indian ex-champion of Greco-Roman wrestling—knocked the door down with a shove. The Madam came running. What they saw left them dumbstruck. The queen had hung herself, from the ceiling, by her feet, an upside-down hanging: slave chains hung her by the ankles to the base of a lamp. She was an albino bat among opalescent glass balloons and quartz chalices. Forming meanders, her hair fell among ceramic reeds, scorching themselves on the transparent gladioluses of the lampshades. The clinking of the hanging fruit was that of a Japanese mobile at the entrance of a monastery in flames.

"Daughter of Poppea!"—was as much as the Madam, ulcerated, managed to exclaim.

"The lymphatic flow"—the overturned angel answered panting—"invariable if we remain on our feet, nourishes and strengthens the ankles, hardens the tarsal sponge, circulates through the phalanxes and ends up developing the nails, toughening the toes, supporting the arch and consequently enlarging the square surface of the sole and the cubic of the whole member."

When they managed to extricate her from that floral scaffold, the poor thing was in such a state that she touched one to the quick. She had lost her sense of balance and, it seems, the balance of her senses as well.

As with all revolutions, this one received a regime of Draconian mustard plaster. The feet gave little way: they responded to ointments with swellings, to massages with welts and eczema. Cobra moved painstakingly on stage. It is true that the role of queen was mostly static. The fallen angel sweated her head off. Her own steps resounded right to her head. The floor boards were drums upon which dead cranes fell.

The itch gnawed at her—"pernicious leprosy"; as soon as the canned applause would explode she'd run to the wings—she had sunk to those therapeutic depths—to splash in a bowl of ice. She would put on the imperial cothurnuses again and return to the stage, fresh as a cucumber. To these thermic surprises the invaders responded with great maneuvers: from her nails a vascular violet burst out which smacked of frozen orchid, of an asthmatic bishop's cloak: beneath a crumbling refectory he eats a pineapple.

That Lezamesque purple was followed by cracks in her ankles, hives, and then abscesses rising from between her toes, dark green sores on her soles. One morning, while changing the nocturnal poultice, the Madam pulled off scabs. Then they left them in the open air, night and day, to the very gravity of their textures. Seeing that this didn't make them worse, they began to believe in Nature and forebade its perversion and meanness: Science.

They burned the *tractatus*,
threw out fetid seeds and herbs,
washed the vases,
scraped the bathtub,
cleaned the furniture with lye.

They opened the windows.

They made each meal "a banquet of fresh vegetables"—Helena Rubenstein; they avoided coffee and absinthe.

They drank six glasses of water a day.

Soon they understood her presumption. The evil was corroding from within. A white eruption invaded them, a hoarfrost, arborescent scab which formed Coptic designs on her ankles, ascended. Malarial flowers, perforated ships: Cobra's feet were slipping into chaos.

The Madam hid in hampers, fled from the living room with her face soiled, and sat on the bidet to cry for hours. The two took turns crying; they began to lose color, wearing away, pickled lizards, lilies of the gospel.

They comforted each other:

"God squeezes but doesn't strangle"—Cobra.

And the Matron, very relaxed: "Have you seen, my dear, what a darling right heel?"

But they knew that they were lying, that the disease ran rampant, that the pustules proliferated every night.

The gods do not skimp on irony: the more they deteriorated, the more Cobra's foundations rotted, the more beautiful was the rest of her body. Paleness transformed her. Her light blonde hemp curls fell—pre-Raphaelite spirals—revealing only half her face, an eye enlarged by blue, purple lines, tiny pearls.

They capitulated.

The two of them, finally, gave in to passive resistance. They practiced non-intervention, the *wu-wei*. Like the ancient Chinese sovereigns they adopted great hats from which a curtain of pearls fell, destined to cover their eyes. They wore earmuffs. Plugging those openings they closed themselves to desire. They no longer touched or mentioned the sick ones; they exiled them with baroque periphrasis: they became the Nile—for their periodical floods—the Occupant, the Unsinkable. Unperturbed by the new symptoms, they came closer and closer to ataraxia by means of internal alchemy and embryonary respiration.

When they freed their senses it was to dedicate themselves to the study of the tables of correspondence. If Cobra nourished herself with dew and ethereal emanations from the cosmos, if she covered her nose with formaldehyded cotton between midday and midnight, pit of dead air, it was to evict the cadaverous devil who had taken over her third field of cinnabar—beneath the navel and near the Sea of Breath—malevolent being, stationed in her feet, who emptied her of essence and marrow, dried her bones and whitened her blood.

The error they had committed was foreseen by Taoist hygiene: the "worm" fed precisely on malodorous plants.

At night, while the Mother slept, Cobra "walked the homunculus." Thus had she visualized, following the *Materia Medica*'s advice, the breath of the Nine Heavens. The dwarf would enter through the nose and, led by the inner vision that not only sees but illuminates, would wander all over her body, stopping for a pause in her feet to reinforce the guardian spirits; then it would withdraw through the Palace of the Brain.

Seeing that she grew pale, the Madam surrounded her with stronger drugs. Around the circular sofa on which she lay, white like a crane, she placed red enamel saucers filled with vermilion, gold, silver, the five mushrooms, jade, mica, pearls and orpiment. On a bamboo tablet, which they divided in two, they wrote out a contract with the gods: they promised to respect gymnastics, sexual hygiene and the dietetic; in return they demanded immediate cure and reduction. With this writing as a charm, the Madam would go up the mountain; standing on a tortoise and rising from among jujubes, an Immortal would hand her the product of the ninth sublimation in a lacquer case; this, duly applied, would produce the miracle.

The Unmentionables were not totally insensitive to that

mysticism. They became damp, tame, porous. They sweated a colorless liquid, rain water which upon drying left a green sediment. In it appeared denser little islands, thick colonies, breathing conglomerations of algae. The pores dilated. The perspiration ceased. Cobra had fever.

One night, her senses plugged, closed to external distraction but alert to the space of her body, Cobra felt that her feet trembled; some days later, that something was breaking in her bones; her skin stretched.

They abandoned hats and ear plugs.
They spent the night observing them.

At daybreak flowers sprouted.

WHITE DWARF

I

"A white dwarf is characterized by a very small luminosity and a very small radius; the radius, in fact, is comparable with that of one of the larger planets, Saturn. Because of this very small radius the density with which material is packed inside a white dwarf is extremely high, so high that nothing at all comparable is known on Earth.

"One well-known white dwarf is Pup, companion of Sirius. So densely packed is the material at its center that a single matchboxful would weigh several tons.

"Clearly the white dwarfs are stars that have reached the end of their evolution."

FRED HOYLE,
Astronomy.

The copartner and the Madam—grey all over, lace mantilla, closed fan, bows on her toes, high heels, pink pompons—got so worn out, so tuckered out,[1] that they ended up finding the juice that shrinks. But alas . . . poor Cobra! All that effort for nothing. Learn, bullheads; cry your eyes out, pigheads. Splashing, sloshing, thus does all daring and vigilance go down the drain.

> Read well, you who strain
> (or your necks will be cramped),
> meditate, self-sacrificers
> and kidney mortifiers,
> Put things right, you pigheads
> who didn't enjoy, while you can,
> ball away, O continent,
> the Toothsome Reaper waits for no man!

(Sorry.) As always, with fags, invention turned into a restless toy; abusive, irresponsible, they rubbed the Damned with it, without restraint, morning, noon and night; for an if and/or a maybe they surrendered to the diabolic reducing exercises.

The rubdowns weren't enough for them. First in drops which they would count a dúo, in soprano, then in furtive teaspoonfuls, they began to drink of the brew, finally they declared it "plain water."

In bed, wrapped in jute sacks—a buttonhole at mouth level —silent and parallel, almost mummified, they would spend the night sucking.

Through the buttonhole a tube entered: a black, rubber tube, connected to a glass pitcher hanging on the wall. Through the mosquito net they would watch the milky potion, the mashed

[1] tuckered out/played out/fagged out/bushed/pooped . . . I owe these expressions to *Roget's International Thesaurus*. Glory to its author, Peter Mark Roget! He's the one I can thank for being a "millionaire of language."

leaves, descend the red scale. They'd smile, close their eyes in pleasure, look at each other, and again absorb from the chin, their mouths heartshaped, in their nirvana, up in the pale clouds.

When by noon they'd already feel that they were drifting, "hollowed boats descending the Amazon," they would interrupt the swallowing beatitude, heavy and damp, soaked like blotters, to urinate—they were so detoxicated it came out pure opal—and to refill the containers with the broth that by now they were manufacturing wholesale, macerating trunks and reciting exorcisms.

"Exactly, reciting them"—the Madam—"but thinking always about something else. Without a doubt"—and she split open a pomegranate—"absent-minded invocation is the only efficient kind. The more you empty out"—she crunched her teeth into one of the halves—"the better your formulas."

Audio: a *fado:* Cobra sings, disheveled and yawning, at the end of a majolica corridor—sifted bluish light; on a wall a map —leaning on a mortar pestle.

"He who believes does not believe"—she continued, Sancho style; "sense, dear tadpoles, is a *product,* the result of a milkshake"—and she waved a fork sketching quick circles in the air—"like any of these watery brews."

She clattered her clog and continued praying and scratching her head. Hanging from the ceiling, clusters of onions surrounded her. The bulbous reflections painted her green.

Cut by the reducing bacillus, the milk curdled. At dawn the basins, and even the washbowls were overflowing with translucid curds, shivering gelatines; in the yellowish sweat that emanated from the curdlings, blown over the emery edges of the pots—rapid sulphurous forkings—and in the arborescences of the casein, the Venerable Lady, a milk reader, deciphered the day's schedule, the density of the nocturnal doses.

To conquer the uncontrollable proliferation, at dawn something was cast out of that yogurt into the tubes; down the drains went little contracted fetus hands. But as if those residues were offered to the gods of the ancient Chinese cultivators, who reward the spendthrift and give doubly to those who waste their gifts, the following morning surprised them with another assault of little compressed jade trees, which spread open upon the contact of water.

"Soon we should go out and indoctrinate!"—howled the Lady Dean—"let's see if we can give a little of this custard to the converts!"

And so their fortunes fared.

Till one morning, doped, out of it, they awoke in a sandpit of fringed edges. Rows of braided bundles of cotton, strings of lint, wool octopuses; in successive waves of pink thread they swam beneath a wavy tent.

Grabbing onto the ropes, panting, with her little froglike hands Cobra tried climbing. She would fall, slip down the jungle of cotton, turn head over heels into the bottom of the valley. She was now white, calcareous, made of chalk dust, she was tiny and lunar, frozen, humpbacked, and compact, she gave off powder. Down there, among folds, fighting hair and nail—wild boar in the burning thicket—rebounding against embankments of fibers, reduced to the absurd, Cobra glittered. The light that emanated was ashen, lacking igneous strips, like a flooded crater.

She rested, leaning her elbows on her knees, fists closed; her eyes were two bulky spheres, each divided by a slit; her navel had grown; her skin was cracked.

When finally, grasping her blanket, swallowing plush—she was breathing through her mouth—twitching and going to pieces, Cobra was able to peer over the edge of the bed, she found herself nez à nez against a little shrunken head, wrinkled and disheveled, that made faces at her from the next bed.

They squinted at each other with customs officer eyes.

"We are diminished"—murmured the Madam, first looking all around her.

"It's not only that"—added Cobrita—"before we were pretty and round; now, frightsome and ugly."

"What?"—the other inquired.

"Frightsome and ugly."

They took each other's hand.

They cried, though tearlessly.

"Let us avoid"—the Mademoiselle uttered, separating her locked jaws syllable by syllable—"like the Alpinists, the contemplation of our nothingness, the fear of the void, the ladder complex."

"The plane of the plain"—Cobra; her teeth were rattling.

"Let us desist from disaster. We must go down to the rug. There the cats will keep us company."

"The cats?"—Cobrita bit her blanket.

"They are friends of dwarfs."

"And men?"

"Whoresons and giants."

The fringes were lianas; the girls, monkeys trained in the sabotage of fortlets, capable of escaping when the shoes of the gunpowder guards in the tower are already burning and the lookouts are fleeing along terraces covering their faces with cloth caps.

They slipped, it is true, they stumbled a bit, they covered themselves with scratches—they were dense and rocky, but had fragile nodules, sand spots. Providence took care of them: when one was falling the other's well-planted foot would inevitably appear, and for the other vice versa, plunging headlong, she would have the one's savior hand, to bite.

They landed on the carpet, shaking off their dust.

Frantically shaking off their dust. Or flinging it off with invisible rooster feathers. Flapping their hands right and left, smacking and whacking their own cheeks, to chase gnats, which attracted by the fermentation of wild weeds, were forming a motionless storm cloud at their present height, and which before, from their enormity, the Shrunken had not thought worthy of chasing away.

The constant buzz, cut by treacherous little whistles—diving insects—stupidified them.

PETIT ENSEMBLE CARAVAGGESQUE

They were dwarfs, but let's not overdo it.

The preceding tale, like all the insidious Madam's stories, suffers from swashbuckling hyperbole, abracadabra rococo and boundless exaggeration. Yes, they were dwarfs, but like any old dwarfs. The Madam, for example, had the proportions—"and also the poise and majesty!"—of a prognathic infanta's lady-in-waiting standing beside a page who steps on a greyhound, watching the monarchs pose. As to Cobrita, let us say that she was exactly like a crowned and rickety albino girl, crossing a company of musketeers on their nightwatch, pulled along by a servant and carrying a dead chicken tied to her waist.

ZOOM

The plunging view gives us the following: along a thick and yellowish rag—a square carpet knit with variant gold threads—among complex unraveled arabesques, into which phoenixes and dragons are woven, following the edges at full speed—newly caged anteaters—the dwarfs are moving. Symmetrical, out of bounds, the one from the black North to the green East, the other from the red South to the white West, both kick along, their ends touching, grabbing demons right and left, now turned into two gauntlets, two autogenous mills, two Burmese leopards catching pheasants; shrieking, terror-stricken, their cracked blind gramophone voices at a thousand RPM.

In bossa-nova rhythm:

"a time of plenitude,
  a time of decrepitude,
  a time of thinning,
  a time of thickening,
  a time of life,
  a time of death,
  a time of collapse,
  a time of erection,
  a time of yin,
  a time of yang."

Yes, they advance, parallel, but in opposite directions. The Mademoiselle—who covers a jacaranda hat with a sculpted Christmas manger—shaking six feet; Cobrita—who, to be brief, is a two-legged Tomar window, accumulates to an extreme anchors and cords, corals and crosses, armillary spheres and Portuguese gothic bracelets—imploring a rainfall of Fly. Frantic, as if those distances regulated the always uncertain rhythm of the seasons or prescribed the harmony of the kingdom, the dwarfs continue chasing gnats. They do, of course, take advantage of the least insect that brushes the other's cheek to give her a slap. They end up purple and choleric, entering helter-skelter and kicking, unloading sparkling cornucopias of interjections. Disintegrated into hoops of gestures, raised hands and blows on foreheads, they conclude the compulsive rectangular course. They know they're being observed, "and described"—the Mademoiselle, naturally—from above. Slow, ceremonious, too theatrical, they move their repoussé booties forward, with the tips of their fingers they gather, how graceful, their silk tails, haughtily they raise their heads, one step, another, good-bye, they disappear under the bed . . .

They lived a long time among the cats they had formerly bred, lice-ridden and eating garbage. That cockroachy world, with its *chiaroscuros* of pissed-on quilt and creaking springs, that grotesque arthritic-styled dampness and those stalagtites of dirty shreds, soaked their bones, filled them with bagasse, caused rings under their eyes: life *underbed* depressed them.

It is known that of all the stars of the Lyrical Theater, Cobra was the Madam's greatest accomplishment, her "rabbit-foot." Despite her feet and her shadow—cf.: chapter V—she preferred her to all the other dolls, finished or in process. From daybreak on she would select her outfits, brush her wigs, arrange on the Victorian chairs Indian cassocks with gold galloons, real and velvet cats; among the cushions she would hide toy acrobats and snake charmers which on being touched would set off a *Skater's Waltz* on a tin flute, with baritonal shrieks. Used to these surprises as she was, Cobra almost didn't react when one midday, upon bending down to pick up a shoe, she discovered under the bed two rather melancholy miniatures. They were wrinkled and stiff, had solid eyes, with moldy hinges. The amazing part is that they emanated a dimmed light, of glowworm eyes.

Cobra picked one of them up from the floor, flipped her over, and raised her dress looking for the mainspring.

"How dare you!"—the shrunken one uttered furiously, and smacked her. And then, automatic, as if she had a record inside, she added in the same tone: "We're hungry."

Cobra never found out—don't bother to tell her now, what for—why she had become partial to—body and soul = precious double-entendre—the two dwarfs to such an extreme, and, if one may say so, to the dwarfier of the two. Thanks to the queen, that pumice stone fetus, that vermin found under the bed, cracked and basaltic, "as if she had ice buried within her, the damned thing," completely dumbfounded, whom one had to watch over to make sure she wouldn't keep eating dirty shreds, began to transform into an articulated and quite human toy. Into a doll, bilious and surly it's true, and in all that regards her mid-night toilette cranky and pesty, for which one had to tape her mouth at times so as to paint her in peace, but when she became more familiar and they allowed her to go among her cats she was quite witty and gabby.

Yes, by a phenomenon of *i.p.s.*[1] which this is not the place to analyze, no sooner would Cobra finish her first show of the night—she'd sing a samba; the Brazilian band had by these hours reached delirium in high; she'd look at her nails—that she would run to her dressing room to look for her favorite pygmy, among cushions and in trunks of wigs and even in the drawers where she'd often hide—her surname had been abbreviated from La Poupée to La Pupa and to the tenuous explosion of Pup. The other one would blow a police whistle and kick and point to her, as soon as she heard Cobra's footsteps in the corridor. They would pull her out from among synthetic pompons. The jumpy kid would slip away through hairy wigs, under sticky corkscrew curls and double buns, among armors of concentric braids and Antoninus hair chains. To hide, hair in hair, when she felt pursued and heard the informer's shrill whistle, she would put on luxuriant horsetails, hats with Marlene locks and even scabby, bald skulls which the miserable poor would use in crowd scenes.

When finally, in spite of her squeaks and fainting fits— she creaked around, like a lobster in a bottle—they managed to save her from the tangle, they'd immediately submerge her in a basin of warm water.

[1] indefinitely proceeding sequences, of course.

The old dwarf would run around the room, building rapid towers with hatboxes, to climb up and reach for bars of soap.

After a good smudge removal, the grasshopper looked white, *the dashing white of the new and impeccable, even in her collar and cuffs,* as if washed with Coral, the modern detergent for the modern woman.

With Pup clean, the ceremony, the gibberish of the redoubling, began. We could, formalizing it in mathematical terms, represent the relationship between both characters as follows:

$$Cobra = Pup^2$$
$$\text{or else}$$
$$Pup = \sqrt{Cobra}$$

An equal correspondence between the Madam and her reduction.

All that she received, all that they said to her, all that they did to her, Cobra restored, repeated, or did in turn to the dwarf. While the Madam—they, true disciples of Derrida, did consider her the original of her reduction, though not for pre-existing: they called her the Expanded Lady—was traveling in India with the choreographer of a Kashmirian Maharajah, seeking red paint for the *Féerie Orientale,* the coming show, the $\sqrt{\text{of Madam}}$ sponsored, as an accomplice, that Borgesian shifting of mirrors.

If flowers, flowers; if shields, shields; if anamorphosis, anamorphosis; if affected symmetries with flying birds, affected symmetries with flying birds: all that they painted on Cobra, Cobra, as well as she could, it's true, repainted on Pup.

"Peroxided giant"—shrieked the one too luminous for her mass, fed up with such bungling—"I'm going to turn into your drooled-on decal!"

One night Cobra lammed into her: she had received the

same, when the curtain fell, in a bombastic row with Cadillac—they tore off each other's false eyelashes and nails, they rolled on the floor; became absorbed in themselves: two witches—Cadillac, the hussy, with her sensationalist and cheap mimicry, had monopolized the ovations. Another night Cobra presented Pup with a three-storied cake in the form of a tower of Bethlehem.

After her midnight toilette and while Cobra stripped off her own attributes, Pup received, grumbling inevitably, the attributes of her character of the day. They divided her into squares before painting her. They enlarged on her skin, or repeated *au pochoir* along a spiral beginning at her neck and ending on an ankle, the *motifs* of a fleur-de-lysed cartoon which formed combinations according to the "optic contrasts" of a HARMONICOLOR disk.[1]

The $\sqrt{\text{of Madam}}$—lying on the carpet, looking up: "Cobra, put more gold on her."

COBRA: "Prepare the soup while I paint her another angel."

Sundays and holidays—Cobra would get depressed—instead of painting her, they'd disguise her. Pup was a little black rumba dancer, a Dutch girl from Edam with a cheese in her hand, a medieval astrologer—a dunce cap on her head; she displayed two fishes biting the same line, she'd push them by the tail, in opposite directions—a cross-eyed Burgundy queen, a dwarf—the humbled maid of a Bengali burlesque . . . but almost always a little boy.

---

[1] Harmonizing colors is a difficult art. A skillful florist, a dressmaker of proven taste, a talented interior decorator, all find, almost without looking, thanks to a kind of instinct, the combinations which enchant the eye; but those who are unaware of the rules which govern color relationships, struggle with overwhelming difficulties.

Harmonicolor allows one to conquer those difficulties, automatically, if one can use the expression. This is based on the following fact: color combinations are always reduced to fulfilling either a *harmony,* or a *contrast.* Cf.: *Harmonicolor,* Disque d'harmonie des couleurs, by Luis Cabanes, Inspector of Design in the Schools of the City of Paris and C. Bellenfant, Professor with a degree from the City of Paris.

It was in this disguise that Cobra wished to preserve a memory of her; in oil, so that people would see it was a lasting memory. They portrayed her, then, stiff, in a simplistic setting, an original by the $\sqrt{\text{of Madam}}$, among cats and other cunning ornaments.

The painter was a devotee of the Lisbon school.

He had been born in Macao, then a Portuguese colony, and skilled in the art of the portrait which does not admit subterfuges—he painted the interior, the invisible—he went over to the West in circumstances blurred by a pious *chiaroscuro;* he had given up his sharp styled calligraphy and his mastery in stamps barely dampened in red sealing wax and writing dedicatories on landscapes of winter plum trees, to adopt a thick and vainly authoritative brush stroke, tending toward pitchblack and the grotesque. He enameled his flourishes with great embellishment, showy little phrases of the tenor "Time also paints," "Technique is not enough," "He who knows does not know," etc. With such theoretical stimulation, and also that of generous fizzes, they managed to carry out an honest entertainment.

When finished, Pup's likeness could almost talk.

PORTRAIT DE PUP EN ENFANT

The canvas is unevenly illuminated; the Shrunken One, standing, balanced despite her big bean, looking at us.

THE MASTER—with a silly giggle, sucking with a straw his supposedly vervain infusion and introducing L's all over the place: *"a river that dries up, a hill that collapses or a man who turns into a woman foretell that the end of the dynasty approaches* . . . He blinks, puts down the cup, and dashes off delicate cherry red strokes, like one who paints macaw feathers, philosophizing all the time, with a dry cough . . . He coats the brush thick white, some light touches right and left: the pleated tulle collar, the silk girdle, completed by a great trans-

parent bow. He wets the brush again: satin shoes, like little
gloves with bows, lace sleeves . . . *Swallows cease to be swallows when they go through winter: they hide in their aquatic
refuges . . . and turn into snails!* He throws in oil, mixes it,
with a few strokes he makes the bangs . . . how well-combed
poor Pup looks now! he changes brushes, with a fine one, of
rabbit hair, he makes her a perfect little mouth, flawless, symmetrical, Faiyumesque . . . *When the radiant days end the
hummingbirds dive into the sea or into the Houai River; during
the winter, which they spend in hiding . . . they are only
clams! The magpie*—from Pup's right hand, he draws out with
a single line a cord which, tipped by the Monster girl's left
hand, falls to the floor to tie around the claw of a black and
white magpie—*is a mouse which spring transforms; when it has
sung the whole summer it burrows and turns into a rodent until
the good weather returns* . . . More dye concoction s'il vous
plaît . . . And with a malicious giggle he hands the celadon
semblance to the Madam, who listens gaping . . . *Everything
depends on signs*—he put a white card in the magpie's beak:
*men do not become hunters until they change emblems and in
the sky the cipher of the sparrow hawk does not substitute the
wild pigeon* . . . Throw in sugar . . . Ah, but what was I
doing? Let me add some cats, for your entertainment.

And at Pup's feet, for her entertainment, three cats appear;
Calderonian, fluidly sententious, they look with astonishment at
the ugly bird: a spherical, mouselike calico, with dilated eyes;
a thoughtful, more definitively bewhiskered grey, and in the
back, fusing into the black, a black cat.

PUP: "May I scratch my nose? And since we're pausing I
may as well tell you to put in some birdies, they're always
cheery."

And at Pup's feet, a few cardinals, that are always cheery,
appear languid and red-headed among the bars of a Churrigueresque cage.

Now, among her favorite animals, as if from a funeral stele, Pup looks at us.

THE MASTER: "Be still. Return to your pose"—how mother-of-pearly he has made her face and hands! Pup is neither sickly nor frightened: it's the style.

He retouches her eyes. A white dot on the iris.

And on the card which the magpie holds, in carbon pen, and in a hurry, he draws a few brushes, a palette, and perhaps an inkwell.

With his steady script and flowery hand he stamps, below and to the right,

his signature.

II

"The American astronomer Allan R. Sandage revealed, at the astrophysical congress now taking place in Texas, that in June 1966 astronomers at Mount Palomar witnessed one of the most prodigious explosions of an astronomical object ever detected by man.

"The astronomical object in question is a quasar that bears the number 3C 446.

"Quasars, discovered in 1963, are young stellar objects, extremely distant—several billion light years away—and very luminous.

"The explosion, which multiplied the surface brightness of quasar 3C 446 twenty-fold, could have been produced some billions of years ago, perhaps shortly after the initial explosion which, according to Professor Sandage's theory, gave birth to the universe such as we know it today."

Le Monde.

There wasn't an inflatable Buddha, nor a life-sized celluloid elephant with two archers on its back, no silk, sari, satin, wash and wear Indian silk nor electric sitar that the Madam, incited by the obsequious choreographer—an ex-boxing champion in Macao, and today, how things change, a devotee of Portuguese gothic art, that's where it all comes from—did not haggle, pillage and carry off at auctions, pleading with hagglers, bribing dealers and cheating auctioneers in the seedy bazaars of Calcutta.

For the *Féerie Orientale,* the dream of every doll in the Theater, she returned to the West bent under a mound of Indian junk where each piece of tripe claimed a fantastical adjective which the diligent metteur en scène pronounced with ornamental phonetic relish, spattering it with sickening Brahmanic references.

What a surprise was in store for her when, cluttered with rummage, she made it to the Lyrical Theater: she found herself shrunken and rather pathetic, toothless and showy, giving affected orders to another ugly and big-beaned little dwarf, as anemic and buffoonish as herself but dressed as a male, on how to sit for an oil portrait among meowing calicos and three plucked and drooling turkey vultures—*Cathartes aura*—who chirped in a cage.[1]

To realize what follows is, in appearance, only yielding to the common mania of mirror-like plots. But what can you do: life likes those crude symmetries, which placed in any novel would appear as unbelievable melodrama, as ordinary, for being too plain, cunning. No sooner had the Madam arrived, Cobra, with the pretext of copying for the *Féerie* certain festooned Khajuraho *motifs,* left for India in the arms of a slanty-eyed boxer, leaving in the stunned procuress's arms the transvestite with the very small radius who had reached the end of her evolution.

The Landlady soon got used to Pup; what she couldn't do, unlike Cobra with hers, was to coexist with her ducklike miniature. The Madam and her concentrated double took on a mortal hatred for each other. For the Venerable Lady to look at her square root which was already fermenting and becoming liver-colored and badmouthed . . . So that to humor her—and so that the idle reader may enjoy the turns of fortune which await the characters of this tale—we are going to eliminate the Mademoiselle, inscribing on a memorial gravestone with inverted plump angels, marble bows and flower vases which would have made even Dolores Rondón envious, beneath Latin scribblings, her withered posthumous monogram:

$$\sqrt{\text{Mme.}}$$

---

[1] Anyone who, upon getting up in the morning, has seen himself enter the bathroom and sit on the toilet, just as he was when he still had hair, or has said good-bye to himself, between two subway corridors, older than a faded postcard, will not be surprised at this coincidence.

THE MADAM—looking at Pup from above, screwing up her face piously, like someone who looks at a rotten black bean: "Now we have to make you bigger."

PUP: "Stop blabbing."

THE MADAM: "Well, you rickety thing, you asked for it by consuming garbage, so now, accept the consequences, because today nobody wants a dwarf, not even in the circus, and it's not in the shape you are, dissipated and ugly as sin, that you're going to become, and I won't even say queen, even only second weeper in the last row on the left at the Lyrical Theater of Dolls . . . So get back again for the change . . ."

PUP: "And why don't you change, toothless misbegotten creature, procuress, witch?"—she stepped backwards to gather impulse and took off like a rocket toward her hiding place under the bed.

THE MADAM—catches her in mid-air and flips her over, shaking her by the feet and slapping her backside: "Clod, devil, mischief-maker . . . Now you'll see how the Master will make you grow with four punctures. Servant! Servant!"—the maid came, she was none other, as was to be presumed, than Cadillac herself in a Mozartian housemaid's cap. "Tie her up and call the Master. You're going to be transformed, you repellent dwarf, you reeking abortion"—Pup spits at her, ripraps her skirt by clawing it, howls inaudibly, like a bat, to kill her with sounds, looks at her without blinking to hypnotize her . . . "Yes, you stinking waterworm"—and taking heaven as her witness—"you're going to be transformed!"

so that: TRANSFORMAÇÃO!

Sound of oiled metallic hoops sliding along a rod. Purple velvet curtains open: my shrunken cockroachy home-movie screen grows larger . . . it is already a vast and very white surface, subtly curved. Yes, my black and white 16 mm—I know: it's really sickly violet and yellow—with worm-eaten edges, interrupted now and then by porous numbers, upside down heads and shaky letters, is transformed into a Cinerama screen in full MetroColor. Stereophonic hymns. On the screen a landscape comes into focus . . . The outline of the streets thrusts something like a black net over the uniformity of white houses, in which hay markets form green bouquets, drying yards of dyers, splashes of color, and the gold ornaments on the frontispieces of temples, bright dots. Grey walls encircle it all, beneath the blue firmament, beside the motionless sea. A great copper mirror, turned toward the bay, reflects the ships. On that reddish orb there appears, in glazed, printed letters, naturally:

Scenery and Costumes
by

—and with the same print, but in capital letters, while the landscape and the hymns fade out—

GUSTAVE FLAUBERT

From the center of a porphyry bowl a golden shell full of pistachios bursts open.

In the palms of their hands, along tile walls, generals offer conquered cities to the Emperor.

Everywhere columns of basalt appear, silver gates in filigree, ivory trunks and carpets embroidered with pearls. Warm perfumes. Sometimes the silent creaking of a sandal. The light sifted by the domes reveals, in the background, a succession of salons. Passing through them the Master approaches, in a violet tunic, wearing red buskins with black bands. A pearl diadem frames his hair arranged in symmetrical curls. Slowly he enters the room: in his right hand, hanging from a black thread, a copper cone.

Fascinated by the oscillating reflection the Madam draws near. Pearl, jade and sapphire furbelows divide her golden brocade dress at regular intervals: a narrow sash adorned by the colors and signs of the zodiac girds her waist. She wears high buttoned shoes, one black, covered with silver stars and quarter moon, the other white, with drops of gold and a sun in the middle. Her wide sleeves—emeralds and bird feathers—reveal her arms; ebony bracelets curl around her wrists; her hands, loaded with rings, end in nails so sharply filed that her fingertips seem like needles. A thick gold chain, passing under her chin, rises along her cheeks and curls in a spiral in her hair covered with blue dust, then, descending, it brushes her shoulder and ends at her chest, tied to a diamond scorpion whose tongue thrusts into the flaccid flesh of her breasts. Two great ruby pearls lengthen her ears. On the rim of her eyelids, black stripes.

To protect her from the brilliant glare that comes through the windows, a raggedy maid—but of course! Cadillac again— opens a green parasol; vermilion bells clink around the ivory handle. Twelve frizzled little black boys carry the tail of her dress, the end of which, from time to time a small monkey lifts up.

"There she is, Maestro"—and she pointed to Pup with her nail: "Enlarge her or bust her."

"Where?"

"There . . . It's that white thing moving on the purple-striped sofa."

"My God, if it isn't a lizard!"

PUP ON THE PURPLE-STRIPED SOFA

It is a circular divan, covered in silk; purple and parallel bands follow the curve of its back, mark a green wall with their reflections. Interrupting them, an amoeboid pink bulk spills over them—the pink of English Bacon: guess why—with big knees and tiny poisonous feet: that's Pup, swollen on all sides, the one who already, to be sure, was not what we'd call proportioned, now not as rocky, nor as dense with matter inside her, blistered, humanized by force of whacks and slaps. They have tied her with small chains to the legs of the couch, by her wrists and ankles. The unhappy creature barely breathes. And through her mouth, at that.

"Let's see what we can do"—with his right hand, farcical, a cardinal or *maja* who leaves the stage with the sign of the cross or the final Flamenco tap of the heel, the Transformer raised the plushy tail of his dress and, hoisting it, drew near the little crucified one. His image diminished along the checkered floor.

"Let us see"—he persisted, rounding his syllables. And he began to consider Pup from top to bottom and from bottom to top, sometimes moving back (he strutted affectedly after each step, as if to recover the balance of his already over-abundant and therefore poorly distributed masses), placing before his eyes his own right hand, rigid and vertically, to study the Runt through an axle, as if he had to copy her in plaster or paint her as the Virgin of the Conversions to then raffle her off in a tombola.[1]

Yes, my dear ninnies, the Transformer is a transformed one, so that upon approaching the little tortured one with his clinical garlic—he feared that the case was one of vampirism—he knows what he's doing.

As was to be expected of her, Pup insults him conscientiously, without a pause and by heart, in alphabetical order.

"What do you think?"—the piqued Madam, who points to her from afar as if she were an upchucked delicacy.

[1] Moronic reader: if even with these clues, thick as posts, you have not understood that we're dealing with a metamorphosis of the painter of the preceding chapter—if you haven't, look for yourself how he has retained the gestures of his profession—abandon this novel and devote yourself to screwing or to reading the novels of the Boom, which are much easier.

"The whole"—the Magician, after catching his breath, ushered in a Gongoristic clause—"the whole is to puncture the *centers,* I mean those vital, enlargement, centers, those of development and expansion . . ." —and here one of his silly giggles escaped him. "If we find them, everything will be fine . . . if not . . . we will have to appeal"—he grew sad and shrank—"to snow."—And opening his right hand, he hurled to the void, with the dignity of someone rolling out a yoyo, the copper cone.

The radiance of the artifact decomposed the figure of Pup into various prisms. Then, the semiological pendulum slowed down in the air—the Master contained his breathing—stopped still a moment, and began a slow-moving rotation over the chained body.

"What are they going to do to me with that astrolabe?" —grunted the scanty one.

"Clean your insides of all the wild Chinese weeds you've been swallowing, tramp."—And on Pup's thighs, with a belt lash, the scorpion, the scale and one of the Gemini were left imprinted.

THE MASTER—the Madam's eyes, fascinated with the oscillatory motion, moved from side to side: the little black boy in a Venetian clock—: "The body, my esteemed lady, is inscribed in a net . . ." —the pendulum rose to Pup's head—"six flowers mark the middle line . . ." —and he lowered it, solemnly, as if the rotations traced the windings of a snake around the spinal cord. "From the flowers, and in all directions, forking, interweaving, threads branch outward . . . The man"—over Pup's sex organ the pendulum stopped—"is opaque, the skein is golden. A dark orle, a continuous, black line borders the figure, which glowing fibers cross . . ." the shining cone hesitated, began to turn in the opposite direction. "Every one of his gestures, no matter how sudden or slight, reverberates in the entire texture, like the fright of a fish in its flagelli . . . Here, see, now here we must alter a flower, a nervous corolla, we must stimulate a plexus, so that it will live . . . It is difficult to explain . . . certain almost invisible, almost unclassifiable beings, among animals and plants, once pricked, grow . . . Give me the needles."

Swift, becoming entangled in her own rags, ripping off with her heel small beads, pearl rosettes and fleur-de-lysed bows, letting fly flaming flocks of fucks, the Madam disappeared into the succession of rooms—it is not a mirror: starting from a middle and flawless point, on both sides of the corridor, Egyptian claws, moldings, interlaced numbers and Corinthian ramiforms are repeated with rigorous symmetry. She returned shortly after, out of breath, her hair unfrizzled; she brought a convexed and smooth silver case which she displayed with the identical surprise of a Byzantine saint revealing an ossuary.

The interior was laminated in fine cedar, like a cigar box. Dull greens, different knots, opposed bands of the same vein, formed an almost uniform marquetry of empty octagons, dark-edged cubes, a compass and several circles in which the figure of a man with open arms was inscribed. On the other side of the cover a landscape composed of minute inlays sprawled out: a wooden Christ, majestic and dying, was entering a tropical city —in the background one could see palm trees, colonial façades, a sugar mill. —The cabinetmakers' cunning: tiny fragments of mahogany imitated the rotting mahogany. Two broads dressed in black, but with violently painted faces, run toward the foreground, their arms opened, screaming.

At the bottom of the box a serrated support held stilettos of diverse caliber and size in place, but these were not arranged in parallel order and along the length of the receptacle, but rather met in a diagonal bundle which, coming from one of the lower corners, ended in the center. Guessable blasphemy— for its simplemindedness: once the case was closed the darts would nail the Christ.

Pup's scream chases away the digressive devils, who were already starting to pull at me from all sides.

The Little Bound Maja goes out of orbit, collapses against the sofa, grabbing on to the edges with her tiny nails, her stomach sinks, she begins to deflate, becomes thinner and thinner, poor creature.

> she flees without fleeing,
> howls without a sound,
> by now she's just a ribcage,
> an ivory bag of bones.

Ivory with sashes—the purple reflections of the sofa—bones striped like peppermint candies, gay-colored skeleton, yes, even the Wretch's support is pretty, even her primary structure, that's why it's not necessary to change it, but rather leave it as it is, something that the fiendish Master and the Madam might do well to understand. But no way.

From the abovementioned bundle of darts, and with the delicacy of one who selects the best pastry from an overflowing tray, the Transformer—ex-champion of chopsticks—picked up between his fingers a slightly curved copper needle, which ended in a small sphere.

He didn't fall into the easy trap of the voodoo nail fetish; neither did he inflict other cheap analogies upon Pup: he did not transform her into a wax figure pricked with ardor, nor into a pincushion doll, nor into an arrow-pierced saint, no; he limited himself, almost with love, with care, to pricking her rapidly, and sometimes only epidermically—he had always had a good aim in puncturing—wherever the cone, in its course over the body, hesitated, interrupted or altered its rotation. He reserved the deepest punctures for the places where the pendular motion had abruptly changed direction.

"Here, for example." —He squeezed his eyes shut, raised

the harpoon, and nailed it right into the groin. Then he suspended the pendulum again, and, always at the same height,
moved it over the little hooked body.

Wetting them in a thick curare, the Madam prepared the
stilettos.

And so they spent the whole afternoon.

"Have I grown?"—Pup finally asked between two howls
and, as well as she could, turned toward the window.

(Upon a bluff sprawled a new city with Roman architec-
ture, stone domes, conical roofs, pink and blue marble and a
profusion of bronze applied to the whorls of capitals, to the
cresting of houses, to the angles of cornices. A forest of cypresses overlooked it all. The color of the sea was very green,
the air very cold.

Covering the mountains,
in the horizon,
snow.)

"Have I grown at all?"—she insisted.

"Not at all"—the Madam replied implacably—"actually,
you have withered. Ah . . ." —and she began to pace, hurriedly, from one side of the room to the other; also wailing, the
maid, the twelve little black boys and the macaque followed her
—"after all that running out of breath, all those break-downs,
all that move aside you so that I can sit down, from a choreographer and two tame elephants, painted Sivaic red and saddled
with cardboard castles brought from India, for your caprice of
taking things orally, for your persistence in becoming more and
more of a woman, more and more perfect, in having more and
more aluminum on your eyelids, you have left me, on the eve
of the première, without a queen for the Lyrical Theater of
Dolls. Who, at this stage, is going to substitute for you? Who
will occupy the queen's blind spot? What jewel shall we put on
the lotus flower? What Cambodian devil shall I dress as you,
and among the butterflies of the *Butterflies and Pheasants* scene,

who will have the nerve to be your double? Ah . . ." —the
maid shook the parasol so that the little bells on the handle
would ring—"who made me squander my savings in order to
restructure you, pull out your scalp with wax and electricity,
with a saw cut off your enormous fingers phalanx by phalanx,
pay for a platoon of ethnologists, massages and paraffin, feed
you with bitter almonds and snake milk so that you'd be flexible
and so that at night your eyes would shine, whose color you
wanted to be, rather than burnt opal, brimstone (goldener and
goldener!), lynx urine, mandarin orange, double hummingbird
. . . until you achieved the imposture: canary yellow contact
lenses?"

"Rest tranquil, oh, Madam"—uttered the Master—"the
morphological change which we are attempting can be obtained,
and without the creature having to abandon Morpheus' lap: we
have only to inject snow into her veins."

Pup shook her head no—a rattling of her tiny cervical
bones.

"Yes"—added the Physician—"the legendary witch doctors
who founded the Sikkim, to combat the white leprosy or *alba
Morphea,* a corrosive tetter, or rather a leprosy which attacked
cattle, injected the cattle with an alkaloid of coke dissolved in
cold water. In the mountains the shepherds used snow. Little by
little these shepherds discovered that the animals, after the
enema, and at the same time they entered a boundless sopor,
grew miraculously, and that this, against all predictions, was in
direct relation not to the quantity of the extract, but rather to
that of the dissolvent. Thus they formed the breed of the yaks,
those buffaloes, tame like horses, which still today roam the
plateaus of Central Asia, following the pilgrim monks."

The night of her first injection Pup dreamed that she was
a princess of the royal house of Nepal: the Madam, wearing a
black hat crowned by a skull, came up to her on a black horse.

They were in a town square, facing a palace of golden and conical towers.

Upon dismounting, with bows and arrows forming symbols
in the air, the Madam, turned into a magician, performed a
dance against the evil spirits.

One of the arrows killed the king.

The magician, galloping, fled.

The Madam appeared on the other side of the river:

white hat,

white horse.

Afterwards, she did not know how much time she spent looking
at her feet.

One morning they managed to get her up. Pup asked for
water.

She was in the bathroom. Behind an oval mirror, a Mongol
peasant woman, opening her eyes, looked out at her, a pink and
chubby hand, with short fingers, over her mouth and squeezing
a bunch of cherries. Her eyelids were swollen and red; her
cheeks: newly washed apples.

"She has grown"—she heard the Master declare, emphatic-
ally, in the adjoining room.

"To me it seems more like she's puffed up, dropsical . . .
and look at her legs: a little wild elephant's. Rubber doll knees.
A fetus in a tube, don't you think?"

Pup drew near a circular window bordered by thick roots.
The city from afar was a heap of grey spots; the whites of the
snow shriveled; the colors evaporated, seen behind a river of
alcohol. Shoots, tender buds which centipedes came to gnaw at,
lapis lazuli amulets, mandarin cornea hinges, heads with black
signs, as if pushed out from within, sprouted on the roots.

It was summer.

She heard the Noise of the Earth.

Upon returning to her room, she passed the kitchen. On the majolica awning she saw them reflected: Cadillac was coming, cambric apron down to her feet, light grey cap. On a table she placed a pitcher, which she had difficulty holding: "That's all there is. Each day we must climb higher to find it and each day more and more has melted. What we accumulate this week must last till next winter, if not we will have to cancel the doses definitively. After all, with the result they've given: a morbid corpulence . . ."

"If envy were ringworms"—baritoned the Lady Dean—"how many scaldheads would there be around! You can see that without rhyme or reason she has grown, you have proof that, though defying the divine proportions, she prospers, and of course, you feel your ephemeral preeminence threatened; you know that at her appearance you will lose all category and majesty and, inveterate second fiddle, from queen you will become a bedaubed usurper, a bovine substitute shrieking in the finales of arias. That's why you exult in the omen of the summer. You think that without the daily frost the Shriveled One will cease her expansion and that, the snowdrifts ever higher, we will renounce our plan of enlargement and development. I'm disappointing you: once the threshold of invigoration has been reached, the body"—the Fury burned her with Lezamesque secretions—"is like certain crocodiles from the bottom of the Nile, if they manage to get into the riverbed they may then lose their caudal fins, because the canyon of the running current, in the shadow of funeral barges loaded with the mummies of children and wooden toys, pushes them to the mouth, where the dew of the air and the underwater humidity favor them."

"Well from now on let her navigate alone! the tips of my toes, my knee, my calf, elbows are all a-hurtin', my arms are full of water, my hands cramped and the crown of my head open, I've lost my laughter, I've lost my color, my lips are cracked and my permanent ruined, I look like a hag, a witch of the popular Burmese theater, and all for the love of art, for seeking among the summits, to help a prostrated girl, the hail of proliferation. The more I perfect my Alpinism the more she perfects her ataraxia; the more mountain goat I become, the more ninny she is. No! Down with the latifundium of sleep!" —and she hoisted a French flag which she carried hidden in her front pocket; she took off her grey cap: underneath was a Phrygian cap.

"Transitory queen"—answered the Madam—"how voracious is your leprosy!"

Etc., etc. . . .

Pup continued along the corridor. She didn't cry. She adopted the disdain of a little Gothic Death dragging along her clutter; a twining retinue preceded her; along the glazed tiles, reflecting sandclocks and scythes, her passage was a parade of skeletons, a pageant of macabre allegories.

She locked herself in with two turns of the key.

She undressed before the mirror.

She placed the Marlene wig and two cloth gardenias among her curls. Of course she had grown. She was a haughty broad, somewhat aqueous it's true, and rather ordinary, with the exception of one detail, which she discovered much later, when she was about to stop looking at herself: she closed her eyes from the bottom up.

It was from all that sleeping with her head lower than her feet.

She tried on the queen's dresses one by one.

She sang Blue Moon.

She drank a swig of cane liquor.

She went to bed very cock sure.

The Madam, just out of bed, blear-eyed and barefoot, a nylon bun hooked to her grey hairs with a string of hairpins, came to her the next day.

"Cobra"—she said to her after a coffee-break—"there's such a thing as too much of a good thing." —And she dropped onto a divan; from among the cushions three calico cats rushed out. "You are as before. Or almost. Winter has already left us and envious Cadillac as well: the rivers and your body have grown. Now get ready for penury. For want. For the frolicsome little monkey on your back."

"Prepare the show"—Pup replied. "Dismiss the Master. Let the summer rain fall through my hat."

She went two days without snow. She drank coconut milk to appease her thirst; she sucked it through a small hole which she opened in the nut with a nail, threw her head back, showed the whites of her eyes. The third night she woke up sweating.

She opened the garden windows.

The trees were adorned with round, red, and polished fruits, so many that one couldn't see the leaves. Among the branches silver roosters slept; from time to time slight tremors shook their tails—a spurt of white feathers, as if they fell from the hats of frightened pages, reached the ground.

She closed the windows. She went back to bed. She heard birds flutter their wings.

Or the creaking of a windmill wing.

She got up again. Opened the windows.

The sea was black.

Among the feathers rabbits frolicked.

From a wicker basket she took out a small pair of scissors. She punched a hole in the Chinese bedspread—with gold trigrams, a gift, dear me, from the Madam. Starting from the edge, quick, voracious, yes, rapid and voracious she cut a straight band, with fringes and all, one strip, another. With the same quick, voracious determination, when she finished the bedspread she attacked the curtains, the cushions, the cute little taffeta hand-embroidered tablecloths with the variegated backstitching in canvas, and the carpet, to be more treacherous she cut the carpet along its own color patterns: from east to west a black band, from north to south a white, from west to east a red, from south to north a green. And while she frantically stuck her puncher into the yellow center, eager birdie with a bifid beak, she clamored with a flute voice:

"a time of decrepitude a time of thickening,
a time of collapse a time of death,
a time of yang a time of yang."

She got cramps in her upper extremities and pins and needles in the lower, hot and cold flashes, chokings and tremors; she blinked with one eye only,

she laughed without laughing,
she had no nausea but wished to vomit,
her only sound was moaning,
climbing the walls was all she wanted.

She carved the dress she wore,
and one by one, the queen's.
She cut her nails,
the four tangles she had left,
the hairs of her genitals,
her eyebrows and lashes.
She was choking.
She breathed through her mouth.
A thousand reeking demons entered her
and poisoned her membranes.
She prayed.

She urinated on the mattress.
She bit the leg of the bed.

Searching for the box of snow she forced open the door to the kitchen. She threw all the drawers to the floor. She tore off the shutters of the pantry. With her teeth she split a flask of sugar—along with pieces of glass she spit blood. She flipped the table over. She shattered a fruit bowl with a nutcracker. She found it at the bottom of the garbage can, covered by leftovers. She had the little key on her. Two handfuls were left. She swallowed them in one gulp. She began to sing a samba.

A good thing the Madam found her. She was a Virgin of Fertility proclaimed apocryphal, a fetish cudgeled to expunge the demons that decimate the harvest: on the floor, naked, showing the whites of her eyes, surrounded by bananas and tainted custard apples, lychees and pears. She was crowned by hoops of broken glasses, toppled saltshakers, red peppers, cloves, clusters of garlic, a ham, big copper spoons and a coffee grinder whose handle continued turning.

"I have failed"—groaned the Dean, whose hair in a matter of minutes had turned grey.

She straightened up the table.

She laid the tablecloth and set her down on top.

She rubbed her with an aluminum swab and then with a kitchen rag dampened in vinegar.

She lit a candle.

Spent the night sprinkling her with hot coffee—Pup's jaws were locked—reciting exorcisms into her ear.

At daybreak she was still alive, though—Beauty is ephemeral—she was already shrinking.

When Cobra returned from India she found her as rickety as ever.

Of what they told her she did not believe a thing.

TO GOD I DEDICATE THIS MAMBO

Like a goose's neck, the envious Cadillac's arm undulates in the mist, plumed white on the gloomy platform. The three are going away, or the two which add up to three,[1] to Moorish lands in search of a distinguished though hidden Galen, the conspicuous Doctor Ktazob, who in crafty Tangerian abortion houses uproots the superfluous with an incision and sculpts in its place lewd slits, crowning his cunning with punctures of a Muslim balm that changes even the voice of a Neapolitan brigand into a honeyed flute, that shortens the feet Ming fashion, Byzantinizes gestures, and makes two mother-of-pearl turgescences billow

[1] [Mme. + Cobra $(+/=)$ Pup $= (3/2)$]

upon the chest, mimicries of those displayed by Saint Olalla upon a plate.

Writing is the art of ellipsis. I'll pass over, then, the encounter of our rovers with four mercenary monks—black background, white cloaks—who in Madrid tried to dissuade them, reasoning with ovaled gestures, as if caressing invisible doves who upon a sash, to give the finishing stroke to each argument, brought in the pertinent Latin, from the mutation to which the girls aspired, concluding, though charismatically intransigent, that it was "violence against the *res extensa,* a gift among the many of the Most Holy One, upon whose wise providence all creatures are dependent"—and they pointed to, on a window case (in the distance a convent, a holy man consoling paralytics), a book with an apple on top— . . . "ergo sin."

I record nevertheless, and with such care, the dialogue which in Guadalupe the Madam sustained with Father Illescas, an enlightened theologian and Jerome's prior.

Having crossed the Sargasso Sea, docile Indians, naked and painted, showing off their bells and little glass beads, arrived in those times at the mountain convent, coming from distant archipelagoes, to learneth to speaketh, be baptized, and die of cold; they brought the gently smiling convert parrots who recited Salve Reginas, trees and marvelously flavored fruits, little birds with red crystal eyes, aromatic herbs and, why not, among such a gay-colored presence, from golden sands the small fat nuggets which the Churrigueresque faith, cornucopia of floral emblems, would convert into knots and arrows, oscillating Mudejar lamps, capitals of Sephardic fruits, Viceregal altarpieces and thick Gothic crowns suspended over plump whirling Tridentine angels.

Cobra marveled at such coarse ornaments and many-hued feathers. She wanted to dress herself with cassava, with tortoise-bitten wood sculpt herself cothurnuses, with tobacco leaves, *caimitos* and mangoes build a tall and gaudy hat like a Giralda weathervane, with Taino statuettes, brittle necklaces and fragile fetish wristlets that jumped like coal dust at the surprise of her gestures.

Pup, a regular Phoenician merchant by now, had given herself over to bartering with the guileless: for death masks and ambrosias she exchanged with popping eyes, in alluring little balls, the moth-eaten pages she was tearing out of a damaged Missal.

But, enough arabesques, let us move on to the medullary subject, to the theoretical marrow of the exchange:

"What folly, my daughters! and from what rustic and debauched minds do you inherit such a pitiful invention?"— admonished the Father when he had measured in carats the extent of the enterprise which animated the pilgrim girls and had raised for a moment the quill pen with which he signed a parchment. Pup, under the table, frolicked with a measly hound. "And, once the surplus pudenda is converted into its contrary and duly buried (as the Church orders to be done with one's fingers and even with loose phalanxes), on Judgment Day, under what guise and nature will the ill-fated appear before the Creator and how will he recognize her without the attributes that he knowingly gave her, remodeled, redone, and handmade, like the circumcised?"

"It amazes me that you think in such a way"—replied the Theoretical Lady: "the body, before reaching its lasting state" —and she observed, with showy compassion, a skeleton and an hourglass placed on a closed fascicle, on one corner of the parson's table—"is a book in which the divine judgment is written; why not, in a case like the present one, in which most evidently in *Writing on a Body* there has escaped a minor though annoying erratum, amend the blunder and nip the erroneous bud, as with infants, when they bore through, one cauterizes a marginal finger or the soft spot on their heads? And it is precisely in this hamlet"—the Illustrious Lady continued—"where I shall produce evidence, worthy of reverence, though to your eyes heretical remedy, because I know myself to be among dissecting experts, and all this skill, I believe, applies very much to the superfluities which thus I would baptize these inconsequential regalias of nature and malformations of the living."

Tucked up among processional moldings, Cobra followed the discussion lying in a corner of the capitular room, surrounded by burnished Plateresque tabernacles, vaulted reliquaries which among thorns exhibited tibias and rotulas, three chasubles embroidered with tiny gems, panels with casks, breads, pitchers of wine and monks in white, and a book of anthems where sirens plunged into the gold of the initials.

Pup, the Costumed Monster,[1] had slipped away among great naval chests and Diocesan cases: in the area where the thorny theme was being debated, she appeared very smily and in full regalia, squeezed up to her neck in an episcopal cloak, a mitre clapped backwards on her head and the puppy in her arms muzzled with a scapulary.

"What baroque mockery is this, shitass, or what blasphemy?"—the Father chided, going at her with spankings nomine Dei to rid her piggish body of the hydrosulphuric demons and vermin which doubtlessly corroded her ganglia and spleen.

Choked up, he continued: "The remedy to which your speech alludes, Madam, has more in common with Leng T'che, the Chinese torture of the one hundred slices, and with the medieval extremes of grafting mongrel animals to lunatics and

[1] See her portrait by Carreño (1614–1685) in the Prado (no. 646) with her compliment: "not too pleasing, but majestic, he has painted her nude, although with features of Silenus to diminish the repulsiveness of the figure." F. J. Sánchez Canton, *Guide to the Prado Museum.*

emasculated bodies, than with the benign post mortem anatomy lessons which here, approved by the Holy Congregation of Rituals and with ecclesiastical license, have been dictated."

"Then you defame me, ponderable prebendary"—the interpreter concluded without composure—"since you seem to find such little sense in them." —And with no sign of vexation: "I will recall for you then, to close this delicious exchange and so as not to keep you in suspense any longer, a precedent which I hope will not embarrass you: that of an Alexandrine saint mortified, in their origins, by the flows due to Luciferian itches of his pudenda, who, in an ecstatic rapture and as if possessed by surgical seraphims, amputated his cockatrice with one fell swoop, flinging it like a piece of tripe to the dogs; thus unburdened he ascended, in a whirlwind of gnostic utterances, to the supreme cupola of the Platonic pantheon." —And between sobs and poorly formed sighs, to Cobra: —"Let's get cracking."

"Then engage yourselves in that manner, my daughters"— the deacon concluded indignantly—"and stir the live coals of this simpleton, since to the same Gehenna and without further preface will you all go, including this dwarf who, though not for being stunted and puny, is more innocent, since it could be said—such ingenuity adds evil to its lucubrations—that she is only the unsuccessful and derisive double of the transvestite."

"Put fire, to me!"—the Madam clamored in exasperation, with a neoclassical gesture—"I shall make of this ambiguous one a houri and even of her miniaturized analogy"—and she grabbed Pup, who began to utter niceties, by the arm—"a plump Moorish girl, since you must know, priest, that if I have come to these godforsaken haunts it is to untie Gordian knots, clarify enigmas, and redress all manner of wrongs."

And with that the threesome marched down the hill, not without first providing themselves with nougat pastes and anise, bread and raisins, blanc-mange, and a few of those meatballs to which Pup had taken such a liking.

In the square, near the fountain, they handed out medlar fruits to the needy and to beggars.

They bade grevious good-byes to the faithful.

They were so good.

Withered, they entered Toledo.

The three of them: with phosphorescent insect intestines, elongated and ascendant like the portraits of Spanish gentlemen —reflections (the learned Madam noted with precision) in astigmatic pupils—with rainbow-hued elytrons, near a windmill met up with none other than Help and Mercy. More than simply textual, they were like parchments and yellowed rhetorics: so Toledan were they that they were Moorish, so dyed-in-the-wool Hispanic that they were antiquarian. Picadors and mule drivers, duennas and maidens followed them in retinue. Their amber silks, their brimstone chattels shined like mirrors. They were made of wings, of white flames.

No sooner had they recognized the duo than they began leaving them for being impossible, so much advice—and all in ballad form—did the Ever-Present want to give them, so many proverbs did they aim right and left at them, since Help and Mercy did not know what a damnation it was not to be able to say reason without rhyme nor rhyme without reason:

that Cobra should trim herself immediately without awaiting further opinions, since in delay there is danger and "better to have than to wish,"

that the Madam should return to the Carousel and there, without further somatic preparations, put on a "Cherchez la Femme" like all the others, since there's no place like home and a bird in hand is worth two vultures in the bush;

that the Changeable would be better painted all in arabesques with an awning of glazed tiles and a stucco dome on her head;

that the customs men at Algeçiras, bloodhounds of greefa,

were going to humiliate them and procrastinate and call them to disappear into the elusive hinge of silver that embraces, though fine, the two Oceans;[1]

that, finally, in this still forming infant, in this soft spot—they were referring to Pup—such raving and metamorphosis was going to accumulate into a pathogenic knot which, when she reached development, would string her up, converting her into a doomed virgin, a blunderhead, or a pixilated loon.

They left them upon a minaret, *dressed in wide floating habits, seemingly made of milled wool, and hoods of fine white muslin which were indeed so long that only the hem of the habits were exposed;* their hands slender and white—stuffed herons—waving good-bye; their voices, high-pitched muezzins, scattering auguries, blessings, go with god most holys.

They all cried.

They marveled—who marveled?—at their boldness; though they held them as daring, witty, and bold, not to the point that they would expect them to venture such foolhardy exploits.

At dawn they saw them move off, weary and dusty, their bundles on their shoulders: they were shepherdesses and mule-drivers. To the south, to the south: outlines of black figures, blurs, earth-colored stains which the reverberation duplicates, dots . . . flat country.

How many days did they plow the plains? What befell them in the sierra? What droughts or frosts did they go through, in what wheat fields or olive orchards, and on the charity or lust of what scoundrels, did they live?

Cobra reappeared some months later, in small rotting letters, on the slangy poster of a Tangerian café. She was a platinum

---

[1] They mistook the Strait of Gibraltar for that of Magellan.

blonde tango and mambo dancer, loads of khôl on her eyelids, a beauty mark on her cheek and two lovelocks.

On her right breast a ruby was hidden.

Her feet were big and her heel was crooked.

She sang a mambo in esperanto.

While the cabaret girl pandered her milongas to a pack of French colonists, groping natives, drug addicts in need and legionnaires, the Madam, disguised as an Andalucian beggar with Pup starving and sniveling in her arms, at the door of a mosque, inquired, under the cover of selling condoms under the cover of selling reliefs with Koranic inscriptions, after urgent signs of Doctor Ktazob, with the pretext of fibroid in the obese one and in herself premature senility, menopausia precox, partial amnesia and undulating fever.

They shook a tin can of coins.

They sang *a dúo* the first sura of the Koran.

Darkened Mozarabic lamps swung with difficulty—so dense was the air. Beneath the ceiling—a star-filled and gyrating sky, with sudden noons and purplish twilights—their paths mixed together smoke strata, slow whorls of mint, raw rum and hashish breath, tea with peppermint and absinthe.

Before a vaulted window which faced onto a covered street —striped figures beneath wicker roofs—and further away onto a grove of palm trees with its camels and domes crowned by the crescent, a squalid Sudanese with an imitation tortoiseshell pocketbook and a magnolia in his hair, presented, to boot, "the zaniest show in the whole province," Cobra: background of accordions, fading light which thickened over chlorophyll green footlights.

She sang with tremolos—there wasn't a night without a knife-fight—wasted and falsetto.

She sold apples during intermission.

From cock-teaser waitress, she stepped onto the stage again for the last mambo.[1] She was preceded by the Dolly Sisters, hormoned twins, a Moroccan boy inured in Indian dance, the Cherche-Bijoux and Vanussa, gigantic and prognathic Canadians who among endless red spotlights and soap bubbles dubbed, never in time, their own records.

While Cobra wiggled her hips to a Perez Prado mambo, the Madam, pillar of the Small Marketplace, was not idle. Following the trail of the transformer she went ever deeper into the maze of the Medina, descending into an abyss of smugglers and drug traffickers. In exchange for news she even made deals with slave mongers. She fell into the white slave trade.

(LISTEN TO UMM KALSUM)

Four long-haired boys from Amsterdam, distillers of drugs in search of raw material—they hid cocaine in hollow-headed Buddhas—murmured to her in a smoking room on the port that the Doktor had been found in a bawdyhouse strangled with a Korean mask, doubtlessly the victim of a sailor left unfinished, in transformation.

A Marrakech tanner, a good-natured fellow with saffron-stained hands, showed her, in the side room of a ramshackle café, his member, and thus seduced and dragged her off to the Medinian cemetery; next to a marabout tomb, smiling, he took out the erect aforementioned and also a curved dagger with an inlaid handle, demanding her pocketbook without further ado and pleading with her in the name of the Prophet to immediately abandon her obstinate search.

[1] The chorus included the Divine Her—a slanty-eyed Cuban launched yesteryear by Juan Orol—the Diviner—who at intermission tossed the tarot, the cards, and the conch shells—the Di Vine (. . . er . . .)—Neapolitan dancer from Caracas, of Austrian ascendance and born in Puerto Rico—and Lady Viner—so-called noble English lady come down in the world after the loss of her tea plantation in Ceylon.

Beneath the whorl of a mimbar a Mohammedan priest sang her the praises of the ex-therapist repentant of his jugglery and converted to the faith.

A fag of the "Festival" insinuated to her that Ktazob did not exist and that he was an invention of the painted "dames" who cruised Pigalle.

In a rococo bar—vermilion plush and gildings—against a wall of pink shells—its air charged with a repugnant and maleficent smell of stale honey—William Burroughs wrote for her on a ticket, in hieroglyphs, the exhaustive biography of Ktazob: enriched by the configuration of new Evas and the disfiguration of old Nazis, the artificer was today a first class "traveler": in the cellar of a flattened earth hut, near the Sahara, dissembling an Alhambra which in turn dissembled a Polynesian brothel with blue-lined screens, red-striped lamps, nude waiters and floor level tables topped with kif pipes that never went out, narguiles of opium and overflowing bottles of mescaline, harmaline, LSD 6, bufotenin, muscarine and bulbocapnin. Given over to the latter, which he activated with curare, the former expert alternated his days between the catatonic syndrome—he represented this notion to her as a little man sleeping under a great black bird—and automatic obedience. *"Son cosas de la vida"*—he concluded orally, with a Colombian accent.

Count Julian conducted her: stands, storage sheds, bazaars, jingling of water carriers, groups of curious loafers, aroma of couscous, sausages and brochettes: a moor preceded them tiger-marked in his striped hooded robe, shiny feline eyes over the handlebars of his pointy mustache. They walked faster to catch up to him.

In a box at the Cervantes movie theater the Visigoth count assured her that the Doctor, a stingy demiurge jealous of his own fabrications, had ended up by exercising his magic on himself: today he was a neo-Liberty midwife with a starched bathrobe down to her ankles, a touch of Rudolph Valentino in her eyes, devoted to her uterine activities and household chores.

Finally, when she no longer searched for him, fanning herself at home with a pulpy palm leaf and helping herself to a daiquirí, minding her own business—what a farce life is—the Madam met head-on with the long-sought informer: in a street quarrel over caramel earrings Pup lopped off a little girl's ear. An intern came to sew on the severed pinna, but discouraged by the difficulty of the first stitches, it makes no matter, he preferred to dispense with it altogether. The surgical prodigy completed, and a few drinks later, the expert commented that he had reached such extreme mastery as the right hand man of a renowned cartilage specialist—Doctor Ktazob.

Without further insistence and gratified by a few dirhams, the second man promised, in front of Pup tied to a chair, that the next day, after the show, the Physician would appear in person before Cobra herself.

They made a pact not to think about the date. Behind each other's back they took Librium. So that she would sleep the whole day, they put a pill in Pup's soup. They knitted. They talked about the bad weather. They confessed a lack of energy. At six P.M. Cobra began to put on her make-up. At eight, in front of the mirror, she was waiting in the dressing room. At ten the bell rang for the first show. She sang a "Cumparsita" without enthusiasm. When her dance number came up she felt weak in the legs. Dragged on by the Diviner and with the help of cognac she went on stage.

"To God I dedicate this mambo"—she muttered when the drums started playing.

She went back to the dressing room lulled by aguardiente, caressing a cat.

At one o'clock sharp she heard firm steps approaching. Someone knocked loudly on the door. It was a tall, thin man, with slender hands—a great surgeon. Greased sideburns descended from a wide-brimmed Panama hat. Patent leather shoes. A button on his lapel. Mirror green sunglasses. Light beige drill-suit. Fat as a chickpea, a diamond buttonholed the silk tie. The eyes:

Cobra: a loud scream: the bulldyke she had in front of her was none other than Cadillac.

"Yes, doll"—the newly glossed Moroccan gangster bragged in a heavy anisated voice, and squeezed her breast—"I've double-crossed evil. Allah le Tout-Puissant m'a couillonné au carré: the inversion of inversion." He winked at her—an Al Capone giggle. "I was fed up with my rags, honey. I went to see my buddy Ktazob"—he inhales the cigar, shuts his eyes, puff of smoke; Cobra: little nervous cough: "he took an Abyssinian's dong out of a narrow pitcher"—he comments licking his chops—"and here I am, like a pimp's shoe: long toe and two-toned. With a few punctures and some slickum my hair came back"—he opened his shirt: Whew, what B.O.!—"Now I'm in the white slave trade. If you want to get rid of the excess, with these rubber tits"—with his forefinger and thumb, as if he were going to unscrew them, he pinched her nipples—"don't lose time in the meanders of Medina: like a purloined letter that the police doesn't find because it's laying right there on the fireplace, like the name of the whole country, which nobody sees on the map, Ktazob hides in the most visible, in the center of the center. Give that tip to the old lady who cruises for you. Ah, and say I sent you, babe; he'll leave you well creased. But, and don't forget this, reserve the premiere for me."

A big laugh. A slap on the backside. He slammed the door.
Cobra dropped onto the bed.
Her head was in chaos.

THE CONVERSION

THE MADAM: "You're going to Ktazob, my dear, as easy as if you were going to the dentist. You think that in the evening, after the benign extraction, without further torment than a slight indisposition, a Biscayan nurse will bring you, along with a bouquet of Burmese orchids, a glass of sour orange juice and your discharge papers, a hand mirror where, rather than your own image, you will contemplate on a background of twilight, with that pallor of a convalescing consumptive, Greta Garbo in close-up. . . . Get off of that cloud: after the butchery and if you can stand it, what awaits you is a rainfall of punctures, tweezings and scrapings, wax in your breasts, crystal in your veins, mushroom vapors in your nose and green yeast by mouth. Cover your eyes with grapes. Your ears with plugs. A yellow dog will lick your feet.

"Rather than into your delirium, look at yourself in the mirror of others: they flee crestfallen, as if they had just lost a ruby on the sidewalk, so that, like Veronica Lake, or like lepers, their hair conceals their faces. By the fire-escapes they enter Negro nightclubs. Furiously they dress as odalisks. They plaster their faces. With blood they paint their eyelids. While the cooks sharpen knives, with squeaks in the background they tire the rabble. Scrofulous and bald like them, an Afghan hound swoons at their side: they inject him to make him sleep. They talk to themselves. They set the table for a dead friend. With their clothes on they shoot up in the subway's urinals. The Indonesian maid finds them seated on an inflatable sofa, in long dresses, covered with flies beneath the poster of Queen Christina: 'Air in the needle, as usual'—and she continues sweeping.

"Or in the operation you feel that the table slopes. You hear a stream falling into an aluminum container. They give you cocaine so that you can stand it. The blood breaks the catgut again. In a transparent nylon cube, they leave you lying naked, in pure oxygen.

"Or you remain perfect, like a statue, until from the wound gangrene starts creeping over you.

"Now then, Cobra, if despite everything and to be divine for five minutes on stage you want to confront this test and commit the ultimate sin, alas, of which man is capable . . ." —she removes the white wig, of weighty years of experience, throws down the ball of wool, from a long jeweled cigarette case lights an ever cooler mentholated Winston, glosses herself with rouge, dons jewelry, sticks a spangle on her cheek, crosses—revealing her genitalia—the legs a surgeon had lengthened Marlene fashion—"then, honey, go down this minute to the avenue on the port, a cognac at the Tout Va Bien, think about something else, take it as if you were going to the dentist, beauty has its price, continue till you get to the docks, you'll see on your left, in the Medina, raised above storage sheds, a decrepit bar:

on the balconies enraptured moors and blond boys smoking weed, go up the narrow staircase that leads to the entrance, a vendor of stale sponge cakes, a singing blind man, smell of cumin, a fountain, a flea-bitten movie house: on the billboard a fat lady with gold teeth and a red dot on her forehead, go straight ahead, to a small market, you'll hear the pustulent pupils of a Koranic school sing, a Spanish boarding house: there you'll see Ktazob's shingle." —She becomes a prudent octogenarian again: "Take the dwarf. I'm no longer up to the job: all that stair climbing."

The most difficult part—Ktazob had platinum hair, was a devotee of the florid perfumed Partagas cigars, and to the branching of subordinate clauses. A slight cough, or rather a strained echo, as of one who must dissemble a gnat's goading on his right testicle, culminated the twisting and turning exhalations and syntactical foliage. A tight black sweater no longer narrowed the stomach's little dome nor the rear and rotund hemispheres. His manners: parsimonious, his tone, despotic; glasses; a cock pigeon's pupils—the most difficult part is not the final formality, a question of minutes, but rather the preliminary apprenticeship, to transfer the pain, and subsequently, to eliminate the sensation of loss.

From a walnut case he selected a cigar, rolled it between his fingers against his nose; closing his eyes, with dilated nostrils he inhaled the fragrance; along the gentle leaves he passed the tip of his tongue: "You must know that I don't use anesthesia. It is essential, or at least my practice thus configures it, that the mutant, in transition, does not lose consciousness.

"If in the intermediate state the knowledge factor of the subject vanishes it is possible that he may founder in that limbo, or that, when coming to, he might not recognize himself in his restructured body. To achieve this wakefulness one must dissipate all signs of pain, which is achieved by algesic transference, a simple exercise of concentration with a distant support, which deflects the neuralgic lightning toward a scapegoat.

"The Sufistic martyrs were invulnerable: their disciples suffered for them."

He picked up a lighter engraved with silver Kufic letters. "If I, for example . . ." —voluptuously he drew the light near the fragrant fibers and, quickly, like a diving kingfisher, or a syringe thrust into the gluteal region, he brought it down to Cobra's hands; the candidate for change bit her lips—"if I for example . . . burn your hand, the burning can pass, shall we say, onto that dwarf in the waiting room. If your concentration, ergo if the transference is correct, I can even pull a tooth out or shred you to pieces without your feeling the slightest discomfort; the receiver, alas, will fall flat on her face, pierced by inexplicable spasms. An Instructor I will train Subject S to learn to emit the caustic darts; another, the scapegoat, to not offer resistance. The Alterer A will be able to practice his modeling force on the Subject to convert him into Subject prime, a force whose stabbing vector will be suffered by, in this case, the altered girlie out there (a), she of course being transformed, by the coaching therapy, into optimal receiver (a) prime. The whole thing can be represented by the graph of the mutation: Diamond."

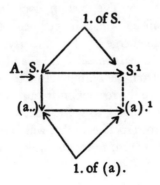

1. of S.

A. S.   S.¹

(a..)   (a).¹

1. of (a).

The next day they began their homework. Early in the morning, talcum-powdered and cool, their hair gathered up in a high bun that is so comfortable, Cobra and Pup arrived at the doctor's office, already imbued with lacquered psychosomatic aphorisms, to receive Doctor K.'s analgesic theories. Among tarnished hypnotic pendulums, stained pincers and surgical knives piled in Romeo y Julieta cigar boxes, with a musical background of Koranic strains, he rambled on about esthesia—for an hour Pup, locked in a closet, has been twisting and turning: the point is to verify certain assuaging fundaments of dervishes —spontaneous narcosis, the visions of interregnum and the *episteme* of the Cut. It was not difficult for him to achieve "somatic identification" between Cobra and the albuminous pygmy who served as her base, but the dizzying filigrees—that the Sufistic metaphysics of the fissure intertwine—were not sufficient to "read" in the milky Liliputian the separate and cold better half of the convert, her double satellized in rotation.

Like everything with her, that's why the miserable wretch has gotten where she is, transference in Cobra worked the other way around: she fell flat on her face, possessed by yellowish vertigo, shaken with vomitous heavings: alas, we'd forgotten that Pup was still twisting and turning in the closet!

"The sidereal emanations of this gyrating weakling are so concentrated"—concluded A—"that she has managed to invert the hyperesthesic arrow. The rotation, doubtlessly"—and he exhaled a whorl of smoke—"has charged her with energy. We are going to have to submerge her for nine days in a barrel of ice and choke her with passive substances, and at the same time hang you, Cobra, from the ceiling with a trapeze artist's gag so that you may achieve the revolutions required, and keep you going with fresh pig's blood, to see if that way we can obtain at least a biunivocal correspondence that will allow us, the moment of surgery having arrived, and if the white dwarf has been sufficiently weakened, welding her to an amianthus sheet, to channel the course of the pain correctly."

Cobra has revolved so many times . . . that tears have come to her eyes. Her tears and that reddening urine—distilled hog blood clots—have left, at different levels on the white walls of the cell that surrounds her, and from the molding up in the following order:

> dripping amber sashes
> opal splashes
> strips of honey
> stains of orange
> twilight strata
> threads tinted purple
> clots of garnet
> once more, blood.

Ktazob looks at the inflamed rainbow. He points out, with the euphoria of one who celebrates the gestural impetus of a Sam Francis, the uppermost, bloody stain: "With maximum acceleration . . . we have here the *red shift!"*—And lowering the lever to OFF he stopped the machine—an autogenous refrigerator motor and two pulleys—which made the socle, fixed to the center of the ceiling, revolve and with it the blood-drained acrobat. He unhooked her as well as he could: Cobra fell, boneless, a bundle of dirty clothes, flat on the floor. She opened her eyes very wide, and her mouth; not even a sigh escaped.

"The worst is over"—the Alterer assured her, knocking her on the nape of the neck with the tip of a shoe—"Now, honey and rest for a few days, to stabilize, with the red indicator, the energy at maximum."

And he went into the adjoining cell.

Charred walls. There, in a sink overflowing with starch where splinters of ice floated, was Pup, submerged to her nose.

Like Allah with the dead children, by the lock of hair he
had left upon shaving her—hair is a source of energy—the
Galen raised her from the Antarctic. Not effortlessly: despite
the bath she was still compact. "Magnificent results in (a)!"
—he communicated to her along with a few slaps—"What ele-
gant gradations!"—From her nose down, the body of the
dwarf, girded from amber to pure white, was a spherical all-day
lollipop for big-headed carnival mannikins. An anemic rainbow
made a ring around her: fading successive streaks became
lighter, dulling their tones to her marble feet.

Pup opened her eyes very wide, and her mouth, she puffed
her cheeks, like an Aeolus, spat a puddle upon the doctor's face.

"Remnants of aggressivity"—strained the platinum blond
wiping off the phlegm with an embroidered shawl. "Next
week"—he added with great cool—"we shall operate." —And
he hoisted an overwhelming cigar whose tip he amputated with
his sharpened cigar cutter.

COBRA'S DREAM

She was near a cracked mausoleum, among reefs dashed by
waves. Stuck to the stones, rags, locks of hair, candles and votive
offerings; cylinders crowned with livid turbans, around the lime
marabout tombs arose.

She made an offering of saffron and flowers and burned
camphor in circles, among chalk and snail marks she plucked a
pigeon, over the turbans she spilled ointments, she polished
the cylinders with a thick milk which, among the rocks, splat-
tered copper-toned crab shells.

At his feet surgical knives and silver lobsters, in his hands
eels and stethoscopes, at the entrance of the funereal mound,
triumphant big shot, Cadillac appeared, looking like Saint
Ktazob. The arch framed him at the midway point of the door;
tinted crystal painted his robe like a stained-glass window. Oars.

Small boats and fishing nets. Golden sardines slipped away among the garlands that adorned it with marine violets. In that niche, the bull dicker—whose attribute, a cylinder crowned with a livid turban, emerged erect from a nest of lace—was patron of the altar of Provençal fishermen. His wide-rimmed Panama hat ——→ *a hat which adorned* the concave mirror of ear, nose and throat doctors; his tie ——→ a phylactery—silver caduceous on black felt—; the jewel shines among ruby auricles and wine-colored ventricles—open pomegranates—bleeding garnets.

Minute golden inscriptions emanated from a motionless white sea gull on his head. His bare feet on the coral on the reefs, a rainbow over the mother-of-pearl waves.

With lobsters' pincers Cadillac ——→ Saint Ktazob touched Cobra. Nude, alabastrine, a tall microcephalic, in slow spirals the pricked one ascended. An almond of flames shielded her; among concentric clouds her little feet, over a field of stars, and equally sparkling, her humid eyes; a Prussian blue mantle, shreds of sea and sky, were ready to cover her; creating in the water a whirlpool which sucked in oarsmen and tail-wagging dolphins, a spout of angels revolved around her. In the quietude of the vortex, together in prayer, her lily-white hands; among the reefs, charred and covered with tumors, pupils encircled by rings of fire, a purplish devil croaked in his pulpit. It wasn't an elephant trunk; bleeding, from his mouth, with balls and hairs a prick sprouted.

Three little shepherds were looking for lost goats—the Madam, Cadillac, and Pup—enraptured, fall to their knees on the rocks, forget the *Ave,* gapingly attend the ascension, raise their arms, touch the mantle, receive a rain of roses.

At a distance of 12 km. from Casablanca, going in the direction of Azemmour by the coastal highway, one can see on the right, perched on an accessible reef during low tide, the sanctuary of Sidi Abd er Rahman. The rock, beaten by the waves, is considered a sacred place. Stuck against the rough stone are rags, locks of hair and other diverse offerings. Around the sanctuary one can see the tombs of pilgrims who died during the pious visit, and a few yards ahead, commemorating a popular miracle, a group of three shepherds sculpted in marble, the work of the Italian artist, Canova (1757–1822).***

DIAMOND

The Alterer's *face is uncovered, smooth, clear, impassive, cold like a newly washed white onion;* a cloth hides the faces of the Instructors, robed in black. Cobra lies naked on the metal table; arms and legs spread out; Pup on an amianthus sheet. On a cart being wheeled in clink test tubes filled with blood. Someone coughs. In the corridor someone murmurs. Receptacles dragged along floor slabs.

ALTERER—"And if we pretended it's a game,"

COBRA'S INSTRUCTOR—"like something reversible:"

ALTERER—"a sound which is repeated?"

COBRA'S INSTRUCTOR—"Man is a bundle: neither its elements, nor the forces that unite them are at all real."

ALTERER—"Cobra, you enter the intermediate state: empty heaven things,"

COBRA'S INSTRUCTOR—"clear intelligence, transparent void"

ALTERER—"without circumference or center."

COBRA'S INSTRUCTOR—"Concentrate. You have learned to deflect pain. Lucidly. I take you to the test."

PUP—"What are they going to do to me with that astrolabe?"

ALTERER—"Take an open-winged bat: nail him to a plank. Have fun making him smoke. He chokes. Shrieks. Give him a light. Take a rabbit: bleed him through the eyes. Take a little man who smiles, tied to a beam. Cram him with cocaine. One by one, bloodlessly—brief cuts in the tendons of his joints— separate him into pieces, one by one, up to one hundred. So that a merchant, smoking a pipe, points at him. A photograph. So that a woman laughs."

PUP'S INSTRUCTOR—"Do you want a doll who opens and closes her eyes, who urinates and everything, with real hair? Do you want a rainbow ice cream treat, in the shape of a pagoda, with a little flag on top? Come on, Pup, what's the matter with you, don't tighten up like that."

COBRA'S INSTRUCTOR—"Think of a very hot sun. You are invulnerable. The windmill wings of pain break against your body. A transparent heaven."

The Master gets ready.

Pup screams. Splashes. Big drops of thick ink flee toward the edges of Cobra's body. Lightning. Rupture. Red branches that descend, forking rapidly along the sides of a triangle—the vertex torn out—over the white skin of the thighs, along the nickel surface, following the contours of the hips, between the trunk and the arms, forming puddles in the armpits, thin speeding threads over the shoulders, matting the hair: two streams of blood, down to the floor.

COBRA'S INSTRUCTOR—"Equally destructive is the exercise of good and of evil. You have eliminated in yourself compassion. With all your strength now, direct the pain toward the dwarf: she is diabolic, needy and ugly, what does it matter what happens to her? She is nothing but your waste, your gross residue, what comes off you formless, your look or your voice. Your excrement, your falsies, how disgusting! body fallen from you that is no longer you. Are you going to care about her, are you going to bother about what happens to her, you who will be perfect, lean, like an icon? Are you going to get blood in your eye for a stinking good-for-nothing? Cobra, the Master is already carving your body. Now he's going to sculpt your nose, design your eyebrows. You will have enormous eyes, crowned by perfect arches, passionate, like those of an antelope who flees in the night, disproportionate: a Byzantine Christ; you will be fascinating, like a fetish. But don't weaken now. Don't let yourself be corrupted by compassion. Overwhelm her. Torture her. I have eaten human flesh and drunk blood. How hateful! You didn't know: with magic she has tried to scar your face in order to take your place. Pins for her: let her bleed. Needles. Coals. Let her burn."

PUP'S INSTRUCTOR—"Rockabye baby. Loosen up. You're getting tight. Don't tense up like that. It will be over soon. Think of a little toy train, red and pretty, it whistles, how cute! do you want it? A bell rings, it takes a fork, it stops at the stations, it goes up a very high overpass, it goes down . . . Do you want to go on a ship? Think of a very funny cat, and now of a baby elephant, bathed and perfumed, who frolicks in the sea; they paint flowers on his trunk. Loosen your little self up. Do you want me to tell you a story, sing you a song? Do you want a cake with candles? Oh, Pup, why are you so naughty? Why do you tighten your jaw that way and gnash your teeth? You're going to break them, you bad girl. Why do you cry like that, Pup?"

The little dwarf neither dedicated her curses to nor spit upon the hooded man. She looked at the floor. A smile of resignation stretched her lips; as with a little crushed toad, the hiccups shook her from time to time. *Her head was turned toward her right shoulder, her two thumbs were bent into the palms of her hands; a white dust veiled her eyebrows, a viscous pallor, her eyes, as if covered by a spiderweb.*

Hastily the Instructor moved away. *He came back with*

*camphor, aromatic herbs and benzoin; a glass of chlorine to
chase the miasmata away.*

Pup's *chest began heaving. The whole of her tongue pro-
truded from her mouth; her eyes grew paler, the two globes of
a lamp that is going out.* A whitish liquid began coming out of
her ears, her nose, and her mouth. A lividness came over the
strata with which she was tinted, from her little rotten feet right
to her head, white sheet.

She was now lifeless, the poor innocent, on the amianthus
sheet.

From his black jute hood the Instructor took out a little
mirror. He put it in front of the festering nose: "A toy train"
—he repeated caressingly—"a little toy train, Pup." And raising the cloth to her forehead, as if rolling up a sleeve, her right
hand bejeweled lustfully, a spangle on her cheek, the coquettish
octogenarian made a bony signal which the Master understood.

The Alterer dropped a needle.

Cobra's Instructor became silent.

From her eyelashes, piercing her upper eyelids, the horizontal wounds of her eyebrows furrowing threads of blood like
broken lips, vertically striping her forehead, two big tears ran
down to the clots of Cobra's hair.

The Master went to unnail Pup. *It was necessary to
straighten her head a little; a mouthful of black liquids came
out, like vomit.*

COBRA—I can't go on any longer. Is there much to go?

ALTERER—The stitches.

COBRA'S INSTRUCTOR—Now, Cobra, you are like the image
you had of yourself.

COBRA—How am I?

Se recobra.
Se enrosca.
(La boca obra.) *

She has passed the intermediate state; she now knows she does not dream; she has incarnated: she wonders which bird.

A radiance of copper iridesces the camera obscura. A murmur of overlapping raucous vertebrae, of caudal cartilage: tiny spheres of aluminum with pellets inside.

Limpid starch or semen, a drivel makes the pillow gluey: shining filaments: Grooved, small rough tongues secret them.

She raises herself.
Blowing and whistling.
Sinuous furrows.
Slow viscous spirals.

Overturn. Swoop. Whack.
She unfolds.
Fearful she touches herself.

She no longer knows if she's dreaming or not. She wants to drink, shout, pull off the bandages, take flight.

Mask of another gloss—lukewarm spangles—eyeglasses of other reptile scales, an iridescent band, narrow in the center, crosses the triangular head crowned by an arch of suction cups; on that vault of slobbering bulbs—his eyes half closed—a young god comes to recline, with the fatigue and serenity of one who has finished a dance: a red U which a plaster stripe crosses, vertically, marks his forehead. With the breathing of a sleeper the striated eye socket contracts and dilates; around him, followed by long white veils, little women with narrow waists and orange breasts fly; silver anklets at their feet.

---

* She recovers./Curls around./ (The mouth labors.) (Translator's Note.)

She vomits a mouthful of poison.
She covers herself with copper hoops.

She is invaded by reddish spots like enlarged freckles, large grease stains identical to cocaine and dirt, yellow fungi of tea leaves in autumn, small Philippine fluvial fish and pus.

She curls around the red columns of a temple of the Asiatic tropics, the ankles of an ascetic, motionless on one foot, the knees and elbows of a corpse abandoned to the vultures in a tower, the neck of a Ceylonese streetwalker smeared with rice powder, the wrists of a dancing god.

She descends into a river—the fault of a rock—from the sky, among chained Fakirs, people in prayer, ducks, deer, and turtles. Toward the waters which bring her to land an elephant draws near with his offspring. On top of the pachyderm, waving, attracted by the coolness, spirits of the air.

She wants to swallow a toad.
The cartilage of her neck dilates—humid ganglionic branches, rings of soft apophysis—poreless skin: her throat expands: oval box where, the sponges of the tonsils squeezed, spurts of corrosive juices and of carbolic saliva will souse the trembling wild dove, the still drowsy hare.

Her tongue splits.

Her fangs fester: green blood.

Without further affliction than a slight fever, with a bouquet of purple tuberoses imported from Rangoon, a grapefruit juice and the medical discharge declaring her out of danger, at twilight, a Biscayan intern presented her with a circular quicksilvered glass complete with a handle.

Cobra contemplated herself at length: "Have you ever seen *Camille?*"—she asked upon handing it back.

¿QUÉ TAL?

Into the stagnant air of the tunnel, the subway train enters slowly. Greased turning of wheels; gears glitter, the connecting rods overlapping. Vegetal orles, cars pass in silence, without corners, their edges like lianas. Horns align aluminum edges.

The train stops now. The brittle flowers of the door locks, tremble. Long twanging series, from a row of silver cubes, one by one the names of the stations sprout; the echo prolongs them in the tunnel.

* "¿Qué tal?" meaning "How're things?" or "What's up?" is also the title of a painting by Goya, on display at the Museum of Lille. The closest to it, among his more famous paintings, is the portrait of the *Marquesa de la Solana y Condesa del Carpio,* at the Louvre. (Translator's Note.)

Diffuse, behind steamed windows figures deep in black felt seats appear, shrunken behind newspapers. A coat, a hat with a twisted brim, a hand which traces a sign on the glass, someone who laughs, a glove, a wave, become sketched in the grey contour of the car.

The doors slide open. Two well-combed boys appear, wrapped in woolens, they jump toward the platform, feet together, looking at each other. Groping for the exit someone advances along the corridor, faceless, in the dark filtered light of quartz lamps, in the dark again, yellow.

An Indian gets off.

The loudspeakers are silent.

Cobra appears at the back of the car, standing against the tin wall, bird nailed against a mirror. *Her make-up is violent, her mouth painted with branches. Her orbs are black and aluminum-plated, narrow beneath the eyebrows and then elongated by other whorls, powdered paint and metal, to her temples, to the base of her nose, in wide fringes and arabesques like swan's eyes, but in richer, kaleidoscope colors; instead of eyebrows, fringes of inferior precious stones hang from the rims of her eyelids. Up to her neck she is a woman; above, her body becomes a kind of heraldic animal with a baroque snout.* Behind, the curve of the partition multiplies her ceramic foliage, repetition of pale crysanthemums.

She waits until everybody has left the car, the departure whistle. Grabbing onto twisted handrails, to nickel-plated columns which open into corollas against the ceiling, tottering on her heels, frightened, mute, she reaches the door. She flees along the platform, between rusty rails, through narrow corridors and staircases with slippery, damp steps.

Between rails and streamers, swaying signal lights, beneath traffic lights with gray fluorescent figures—fur coats—standing on traffic islands the wearers of numbered helmets point to her; beggars laugh at her; enveloping her in their breath, drunks follow her. She walks against walls, wrapped in a black cape, covered by a cardinal's hat, crestfallen, as if she had just lost a ruby, so that, like Veronica Lake or a leper, her hair conceals her face.

On the ground clochards are sleeping on their vomit; they awake to sing an aria. On white canvas chairs, tall, exposed like mechanical dolls—little heads protected by linen hats—blind men play arias on their worm-eaten, wall-colored accordions.

The songs pursue her, and the fluted blowing of the mother-of-pearl inlaid boxes enlarged by the dark.

A filthy beggar woman, tatters strung with trinkets, comes up from behind, on tiptoes, a scream, she tears her cape. They pull off her hat. The cackling resounds in the cavern, interrupting the blind men's monotonous ballad, interrupted by the successive banging of subway doors.

She disappears among mute maps,

> Fused fluorescent tubes,
> stuck revolving doors,
> upside down arrows,
> collapsing ramps,
> passages with no exit,
> puddled urinals,
> distributors of stale pastries,
> vendors of worm-eaten newspapers,
> carnivorous flower stands,
> cableless elevators,
> telephones without lines,
> drugged policemen,
> crazy shoeshine boys.

//Behind the fading light sifted by shells of yellow quartz, sketched in the interval left by the grey tops of cars, the street; among branchings of iron and glass, her orange hair: Cobra with the station masters// a purple blinking neon M that is growing// near barefoot beggars—their scorched, humped feet occupy the foreground—an orange light sketches her too neatly among tatters of red cloth and bread baskets. In the dark, one can barely distinguish the profiles, the objects—a glass pitcher full of wine, a lute—the gestures// in the street.

It is night. It rains. Water striking against asphalt. Behind the rain people pass, outlines blurred; beneath the striped halo of street lights, blue rectangle, the store windows frame fruit baskets full of apples, pastry bowls dripping honey, kitchen boys with starched white caps, iron ovens where, stuffed with almonds, surrounded by laurel wreaths, whole animals revolve.

Protected by a nebulous god—the thick smoke coming out of inns—Cobra crosses the street. Behind remains the opening, in the middle of the sidewalk, its stairway sinking down, ceramic reeds that rise, fork, curve around, envelope the sign of the METRO.

The rancid vapor of the chophouses, the stench of burnt meat, sour alcohol and fat: the acid of the rain that works upon her, corrodes her.

She took shelter under the marquee of a theater. On a corner, among stucco pergolas, panels with balconies in bas-relief, gilded merlons and a gondola, there was a photomaton. Inside the machine—having drawn the black curtains the flash had worked by itself—before a mirror flashing light, she was able to register the damage: the severe scaffolding of her hairdo crumbled on all sides, the curls—vanquished springs—dripped bleach, over a forehead tripe bows fell, a large black stain rolled down from her eyes, the blue shadow emerged around her mouth.

She came out crying.

A little boy stared at her.

An old man remembered Theda Bara.

A cat followed her.

A Portuguese bricklayer inhaled her perfume.

Radiating a neon daylight, the transparent cubes of show windows advanced at intervals over the sidewalks. Inside them, inserted into the fixed scenery, in the darkened theaters of their rooms, whores lay naked among purple cushions, on lynx skins, cuddled in vast wicker chairs whose backs formed a circle of Moorish stars around their heads; paper flowers, bottles of crème de menthe, Danish magazines and small monkeys surrounded them. Their servants—Jamaican eunuchs—rubbed the dampened glass of the windows with flannel; the sailors knocked from the outside with their knuckles.

They were the ones who saw Cobra.

People started crowding around her.

They followed me.

They harassed me.

They chased me up against a wall.

Black spangles on her cheeks, lustful rings on her fingers, dart of jewels on the grey-haired pompon, from the group emerged a grease-painted octogenarian. She strutted near, singing, with a nasal twang, in falsetto: "¿Qué tal?"—she asked, imitating me.

Her bony forefinger very close to my lips, she shouted: "It's him."

COBRA II

THE INITIATION

EAT FLOWERS! I AND II

FOR THE BIRDS I AND II

WHITE

INDIAN JOURNAL

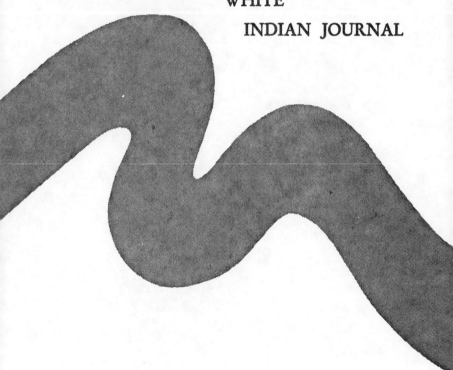

THE INITIATION

He had wandered along the street of show windows—among purple cushions, on lynx skins, cuddled in vast wicker chairs whose backs formed a circle of Moorish stars around their heads, whores lay naked—sipping anise in old bars, beside flower-belled gramophones.

Not daring to enter, he had passed near the little door, beneath the wrought iron insignia—a coach.

DRUGSTORE

He saw himself in a mirror, surrounded by a drawerful of disheveled scarves, a plastic sphere filled with water—in the back, bubbles, several watches—ties with golden branches and another mirror, where he appeared backwards. It caught the image of his hand among the fabrics—attentive to the saleslady's movements—opening the buttons of his jacket, stuffing the black scarf inside, against his chest. He leafed through a magazine. He was sweating. He turned around absent-mindedly, leisurely. He smoothed his hair, with his knuckles he caressed his beard, he adjusted his belt, dusted the chamois leather of his boots. Little by little he pulled out the wool band. He ripped off the price tag. He tied the scarf around his neck. A black sash girded his chest, the other fell from his shoulder to his waist: the saint of a Ravennese mosaic, phylactery of black stones.

He bought a newspaper. He unfolded it, leaning against a column which open hands engulfing celluloid globes joined to the ceiling. Oval shields with eyes and lips for coats-of-arms hung from the walls; on curved-legged tables silver muses danced: the trains of their gowns were flower vases, and their heads, decorated with butterflies, lamp fixtures.

copenhagen   brussels   amsterdam*

Outside, beneath palms of an acrylic green, a mulatto woman dances. Over the sand, orange light; kites over the black bands of the sidewalk.

appel   aleschinsky   corneille   jorn*

He put the newspaper, folded, on a pile of magazines. He picked it up again taking one.

Undulating corridor of mirrors.

poisonous snake of India*

Plexiglas flowers open. The same record in English begins again. Vinyl circles overlap. Hum of Japanese movie cameras. Double images. Reflection of symmetry. Multiplication of reflection. Repeated photographs, overexposed. On the whiteness of a book cover, a porcelain head covered with black ideograms.

Volumes of bakelite. Intersection of edges. He knew he was going to find them.

> *he receives his wages in the paymaster's office.**

Empty sequences.

IN THE BAR

Now he moved along the corridor, over a black carpet which hid a net of tigers and white letters. Almost without realizing, he had opened the little wooden door. He felt his own breathing, his footsteps, the arches of his feet light upon the tapestry, heel to toe. Near the animals, smearing the white of the letters, the traces of his steps were caught for a moment, in the tangles.

At the end of the corridor, in a corner which received the diagonal precision of the bar, in front of a black chalk drawing projected upon the back wall, TUNDRA appeared. As he moved, black lines fled across his face, across the edges of his body. *A-13470, Los Angeles, Calif. USA. Good-looking man of 33, height 5'10″ (photo and particulars available); interested in meeting a good-looking, well-built, education-minded, dominant male, possible motorcycle-type leather fan. Photo and sincerity appreciated (and if in L.A. area, a phone number).* Cracked black leather. His dirty, straight hair fell in tangles to his shoulders. *A-13486, New York, N.Y. USA. Handsome male of 30, of docile nature, well-built, wishes to meet or correspond*

---

* anagrams and synonyms (or hypographs) for COBRA: 1) COpenhagen BRussels Amsterdam; 2) appel aleschinsky, etc., a school of artists centered in these three cities, known as the COBRA group; 3) poisonous snake of India = Cobra; 4) he receives his wages in the paymaster's office = the verb *cobrar* and thus cobra, third person singular conjugation of this verb. Cobra is also the name of a singer who died in a plane crash over Fujiyama, and the name of a motorcycle gang that frequented St. Germain des Près. (Translator's Note.)

with boot-wearing men interested in the subject of discipline, levis, boots, belts, leather clothing, uniforms of all types: would like to meet and correspond by letter or tape with dominant men interested in these subjects. At his waist, welded to a chain of forged links, a tin rosette. *A-13495, Vancouver, B.C. Gentleman of 40, of dominant nature, very sincere and understanding, with varied interests, would like to meet slim man between 20 and 45, not over 5'8" tall, of docile nature and interested in the subject of discipline. Also would like to hear from "Foot Adorer" in issue of November 25th.*

"We were waiting for you." —And he turned around. He wore his name on his back, tattooed in the leather, dull black upon the shiny black of the hide.

In the drawing projected on the wall two men were fighting. Or not. The blanks formed other figures: the same men jumped toward each other, but to embrace, naked.

"It's a good thing you came. Today's the day. Because to be a leader you have to pass through submission, to gain power you have to lose it, to command you have to first lower yourself as far as we want: to the point of nausea."

SCORPION wore around his neck a funeral amulet: in its middle circle, protected by two pieces of cut glass, surrounded by amber beads, little porous bones with filed edges were heaped —baby teeth, bird cartilage—bound by a silk hatband, lettered in black ink and gothic capitals with German names.

On his wrists, eagles with blue dots. His boots, untied.

/Bleeding skeletons stick to caryatids. Burning bodies. Ashes. White mausoleum. Shrouded in brocades and coarse jewels, toward the towers they escort the dead infant.

From TOTEM's coat dangled little bronze cymbals, bells with broken clappers, dented cowbells, Mexican jingles. His straight eyebrows were joined, his high cheekbones, yellow. Torn pants, mended with patches; in the pockets penknives and glass; from a sweater tied to his waist, sleeves hung down to his knees. A rattling of junk, the rusty creaking which announces a row between Chinese shadows, the apparition of a devil in the Indonesian theater, the tumble of a monkey acrobat, measured his gestures.

/Sudanese soldier. Abyssinian water carrier. Horse rider from Ethiopia. Pitch black body, smooth and shiny, grape-colored pupils. He drinks from an ox horn and pours over his genitals an opaque and acidulated mead. Face down, he rubs his tense frenum—*masenko* fiddle string—his bulbous, purple glans against a buckskin stained by cum. He turns around. Starchy puddle on his belly. Laughter. A little twangy song. Eating sorghum bread. In the corners of his mouth, and of his eyelids, the sign of monsters.

Behind shelves of bottles, opaque screens, and the curves of Turkish stools, a light filtered by algae emerges from the bottom of the aquarium which occupies an entire wall of the bar; slow shadows—vibrations of tiny wings—blur that neon daylight submerged among stones and white polystyrene coral, beneath motionless sea horses of fluorescent glass and lily-white rustproof flowers, always open.

In front of the light which gushes from the water, where the shadows of fish are black butterflies, TIGER dances, smokes, hits himself, inhales again, impelled by the kif he jumps, bursting Tibetan necklaces, diagonally into mid-air. Now he runs circles around me, looking at me. Underwater transparency. Looking at me. Hothouse light. I revolve too. Glass on the floor. Looking at each other. He bangs on the glass of the fish tank with open hands. Slow, flat, lanceolated animals, open symmetrical leaves with tenuous nerves, hurry back and forth. Streaked with mercury. Mayan faces. Their glowing orange flagelli follow, entangle them.

I am smoking. The weed is blowing through my ears. I

am running circles around them. Looking at them. They are revolving too. A glass breaks.

/Behind the bar three naked women appear, gilded.
The fish have clouded it all.
Behind the wall zebras are fleeing.

TUNDRA: "We will assign you an animal. You will repeat his name. La boca obra."

SCORPION: "So that you'll see that I am not me, that one's body is not one's own, that the things that make us and the forces which put them together are passing fancies"—and he cuts the palm of his hand with glass, then rubs it against his face; he sucks his blood (laughing).

/The burning bodies, blue corpses burnt to ashes, brimstone feet and eyes shrouded with mushrooms, fall into the white, still river. Into the river, somersaulting in the air; into the still water the cremated, the leprous fall. Among gurus who pray, gods who give out rotten oranges, and children who beg, bones in flames fly over the astrologer's choir loft, into the water that doesn't move, and also rotting genitals, corroded faces, slashed hands: blood clots. Along the banks, flames, the cries of gongs, the night.

TOTEM paints on his chest, over his heart, a heart. He dances and smears himself with scarlet. A snake shines phosphorescently on him, curled around his phallus. Its soft head sticks on to the glans. Sharp, dripping cum, the little tongue penetrates.

TIGER: "In a dream I saw myself walking past a tent crowded with boots, shoes, mountings and buckled straps, but those objects were not made like ours, and their material, instead of leather, seemed like dry and sticky blood. I told it to the Instructor: 'A total absurdity,' he said to me. Later, when I saw them, I understood that they were objects that westerners use."

And he bangs on the fish tank again. And to the puzzled bartender: "What's the matter? Don't you like it? Do you want me to say a word, a syllable and turn you into a bird? Do you want me to conjure up five thousand minor demons right this minute, to prick you, to poison your precious body fluids? Make me a gin and tonic."

/Behind the aquarium—black stripes ripple when the water moves, through the white, fish glide—zebras continue rushing. Chessboard loins. Viera da Silva loins. Parallel bands spread behind the glass, skulls, necks which cross, tails, manes which open in slow motion, lips discharge strings of silvery drool which dash against the glass; parallel bands which shrink, seen in a concave mirror. The galloping sound, muffled by sand, by water, mixes with the percussion of the orchestra; its rhythm is the banging on the fish bowl. The zebras leap in files, at regular intervals, a file of black zebras striped white, a file of white zebras striped black; they reach the top—the height of the water—they fall, front legs bent, they rise and flee in disorder while another file behind the glass rises, flies.

On another wall in the bar, in black and yellow dots, a blonde cries—her tears are enormous—; in a bubble, gushing from her lips, the words *"That's the way it should have begun! but it's hopeless!"*

We went out.

Everything had changed.

The corridor was white.

On the floor, skull-goblets, femur-flutes, striped scepters, swastikas, wheels, were arranged in an indecipherable order among cubes of a rainbow-hued glass.

The street door opened automatically.

We could barely stand the night's glare, the noises reverberated in our heads. The motorcycles were lying on the side-walk. It was raining. In the square one could hear the guitar-strumming of the inns, far-off. At the subway entrance a frightened woman appeared. She was wearing a red hat; its ribbons, falling from the brim to her black cape, hid the gold flowers on her face. Her make-up was violent, her mouth painted with branches. Her orbs were black and aluminum-plated, narrow beneath the eyebrows and then elongated by other whorls, powdered paint and metal, to her temples, to the base of her nose, in wide fringes and arabesques like swan's eyes, but in richer, kaleidoscope colors; instead of eyebrows, fringes of inferior precious stones hung from the rims of her eyelids. Up to her neck she was a woman; above, her body be-came a kind of heraldic animal with a baroque snout.

We're moving now—in the suburban silence the rumble of motors; over yellow bands, black flashes—on our motorcycles, at full speed. No hands, we shut our eyes, we pass—an alarm bell—under the barriers. Zigzag between crossing locomotives: from open train windows handkerchiefs come out, straw hats pulled by the wind, a girl shouting. Our wheels don't touch the ground; on the asphalt arrows pass, in enlarged letters, names of cities, numbers.

TUNDRA repeats a formula, flings a bottle which breaks against the pavement: green spot; SCORPION accelerates, takes off his helmet: "the skull is a casket: let my brains spill over the road!"; TOTEM hugs him by the waist, braces his head against his back, TIGER opens a hand and in the air a strip of sulphurous powder remains, spreading, unfolding; orange strata, fluorescent cumulus clouds: chemical twilight. We take off, yeah, we rise, higher, higher: we are flying!

Sounding sirens, in pursuers with ultraviolet headlights, with poisoned arrows and crossbows, bottles of bacteria and ballistas, the greenish agents of the orgy patrol follow us—

monstrous syringes—waving night-sticks of war, miniature lasers in each cavity, macromolecules in their ears.

> We turn at every corner,
> we blow up the bridges behind us,
> we turn traffic signs around,
> we spray nails and blazing phosphorus,
> we make traffic lights red.
> Thrice do we paint the raging sea.
> With the triptych we close off the street.

To urge them to turn back, TUNDRA delivers a speech to the pursuers. He translates it into every language alive and dead: when he's going through Sanskrit they respond with a tactical atom bomb: the BOOM makes the earth quake.

SCORPION blocks their way with pyramids of skeletons which stir and creak like crabs; he shows them, on a magnificent neck chain, their heads spitting coins.

TOTEM writes on a kite: FATE L'AMORE NELIA GUERRA and flies it high; from the tail condoms and bells fall.

"Stop!"—TIGER shouts—"or I'll stamp my foot three times and make an army of gigantic cats rise up and charge against you!"

And he stamps his foot three times: out of season and place, flowers sprout everywhere: sandalwoods and white lilies bud on the enemy motorcycles; gardenias on the handlebars, white orchids on the exhaust pipes and big sunflowers which paralyze them by becoming entangled in the wheels. The foliage covers the cops, remains of petrified pursuers; the weapons have been caught in creeping ivy, taken, hooked in the green tangles. The vice squad, in its frozenness, is already a snapshot, a photostat copy of the primitive squad, a wax museum, a gathering of cardboard demons, the abandoned props of a cheap circus which are disappearing among the weeds, in the dust, into the ground, which no one remembers and are only visible by the darkest green of their shadows, in certain aerial shots, taken at twilight and after the snow.

THE RUINS

The archaeologists studied them by deciphering the shadows, believing they were from a Roman theater.

Others suggested an Indian observatory with its hourglasses, sundials, telescopes, celestial charts, and astronomers viewing Orion, draped in a tapestry of fossil shells—proof that the sea had once invaded it and that in another era it had been embalmed in a river of lava.

They dug them up.

With the weapons they founded an arms museum.

They filmed them in Cinerama.

Planeta devoted an issue to them,

Coco Chanel engaged them for her winter fashion show.

From everywhere tourist caravans stream.

Straddling the sergeant's head, a little boy eats a strawberry ice cream cone.

PRAISE AND GLORY TO THE VICTORS
TO TUNDRA

Your locks are golden and around your body an orange halo glows; you sleep upon the tree of Rhetoric: your voice is the unit of all sound, your body, which rocks the leafy treetop, is the standard of human form: your height is exactly eight times your head, your eyes are perfect ovals and around your navel a circle defines the curve of your hips, the gothic arch of your thorax, and the implantation of hairs in the hollow of your pubis;

at your footstep one hears music of the five-tone scale, the trees bend to give you shade;

you walk leisurely.
By the way you moved your right foot I knew you were a god.

TO SCORPION

To the gems, pastries, and toys with which we have filled
your barge, we add new offerings. To favor your voyage, close
to your body, which the damp adorns with tiny flowers and
which is cloaked, from your feet up, by lichen veils, we place an
Ibis, a pineapple, several coins and a chart of the river, a stone
fallen from the moon, another which will make you dream, and
another, yellow like lynx urine, which will be clear or cloudy
depending on whether you are happy or sad.
We know you will return.
We shall wait for you in the murmur of the night that precedes
the river's flow.
Our emblem shall be the bird you become.
You are the jaguar that springs toward the summer sky and
turns into a constellation.
We lick the pus, the wax from your feet.

TO TOTEM

Your phallus is the largest and on it, as upon the leaves of
a sacred tree of Tibet, all of the Buddhist precepts are written.
Without having been ciphered by anyone, starting in spiral for-
mation from the orifice, the signs of every possible science are
inscribed around the head. Your buttocks are two perfect halves
of a sphere; we come to trace purple and gold concentric circles
upon them, and to pour ointments over your hands.
Look at us.
We have covered your bed with striped orchids,
the chamber with Persian tapestries, pillboxes, fruits, and astrolabes. So that you come to inhabit them with your laughter.

TO TIGER

Your mother bore you beneath a tree: from her belly you leapt to the ground; where you fell a giant lotus flower, of every color, burst forth.
You pronounced a name:
on your left and on your right two cascades spouted, one of cold water and one of hot; four gods descended to shower you.
Your name, recorded on an aerolite.
You enter the water without wetting yourself, the fire without burning yourself; you walk over clouds and mist.
At the passing of your horse the forest opens.
Sacred monkeys, elephants, and disciples follow you in caravan.
If you command
a rain of stars will fall at once over the earth.

THE PARK

Over the tiles of a poplar grove the motorcycles glide, between gazebos cracked by dog-chewed mint sticks, dry roots. (Through the crevices white lizards slip away.) We accelerate, we brake suddenly: skid, capsize, rapid hoops of mud. Bell-flowers close, the dark green tangles around broken capitals, unfinished marble heads, upside down on the ground, tremble. Armadillos curl up beside the whorls; frightened hares flee through stone ducts. From left to right. From right to left. We circle a dry fountain until we're dizzy. We urinate in the mouths of dolphins: the porous stone drinks the yellow stream they vomit, foaming drivel.

We strip a small wood of willow trees.
We rain pebbles upon a ridge.
The park: a burning embankment, beneath the humus.
Pollen in flames. Black grass.
Ashes consume the last branches.

Plain razed by night beasts to sea level, cyclone, napalm.
Over the white even surface, fossil flowers.

We continue toward the outskirts. Identical avenues. On either side unfinished gothic castles of reinforced concrete pass, a second before collapsing—in the oval windows, ladies of stone—churchless towers whose electric bells toll the Angelus, gas stations, lamp stores, parallel lines of blinking yellow lights, smoked glass crematories. Under the silver-plated signs of Esso and dripping oil tanks, sitting on the ground among wax mannikins, families spread flowered blankets over the mustard grass. "A nice day!"—they comment with their walkie-talkies—they open Coca-Colas and cans of herring.

Naves lie at ground level, the neon brilliance of hothouses.
A dam.
An antelope crosses the highway.
We are going into a forest.
We have left the motorcycles and are walking along a narrow path, sheltered by dry branches. In the distance, the hum of the highway. On the ground, among black feathers and snake scales, mixed with pebbles, perforated, drooling eggs break against the palisaded sides as we pass; biting the rushes, bathing them with their thick saliva—blurred pupils—iguanas, fierce chameleons watch us; in the brush, snakes battle: we hear panting, overturnings in the hay, torn membranes, creaking cartilage, splitting fangs; we hear cooings, seeds rupturing, cottony flowers opening, sap rising, buds sprouting. We hear our breathing, the murmur of the night, the wind.

I am afraid.
We come to a clearing.
Silence. Laughter. A bird passes.

TUNDRA: "Now you pass over to the other side: Look."
—And he opened a box in front of his face.

A drooling animal jumped on me, with cold paws, his toes stuck to my cheeks, like suction cups.

The jack-in-the-box jumped on him, sounding its toy croaker. Out of the box came springs, a stream of water, a little key from one of the frog's legs. SCORPION wound it up again. TOTEM wet his lips with beer, helped him undress. With open arms and an unraveling skein of hemp rope placed on his right arm like a bracelet, TIGER started to run around him.

Tied to a tree.

Triangles of bindings on his chest.

Two bloodied furrows swelled his knees and fists, cut into his ankles.

They stepped back to look at him.

"Not bad"—said TUNDRA. "Set the camera."

Flash: icon lacerated by infidels// white fang mask against the white fungi of the tree// ashen actor who bends under the weight of his ornaments and falls over a drum// plaster death mask; conjurings in green ink.

SCORPION: "On your guts, on your rotting liver enormous pale butterflies will come to rest."

TOTEM: "You will drink of my blood"—and he poured a bottle of ketchup over him—; "of my cum"—and he opened a container of yogurt over his head.

TIGER: "I am going to blind you"—a flash, in his eyes.

It wasn't Indian music. It was the Beatles.

It was Ravi Shankar. The timbrels served as background for a Shell commercial. TUNDRA repeated yawning "You have gone through submission, you have lost power, etc." Another raga followed the pause that refreshes.

SCORPION: "Now what, do we kill him?"

TOTEM: "He has to be fucked."

TIGER: "No. Let him loose. He's to get dressed now."

TUNDRA: "He needs a name."

SCORPION untied him pulling the bindings to break them, cutting them with a knife against the skin. TOTEM took his hand and put it on his penis. He wet his index finger with saliva and caressed his lips. He blew into his ear. TIGER stirred a mill of noon prayers.

TUNDRA dipped the paint brushes.

SCORPION sketched on the back of his jacket a vertical arch which opened in the hide, dripping, soaked in by the plush, writhing like a mangled snake.

TOTEM, who slept among the stones—drunken god upon a miniature landscape—jumped up: with a single stroke, expert penman with an angular style, he drew the circle of Divination, twisted over itself and edgeless, the perfect hoop. With a stone seal TIGER stamped beside the circle a square mark: BR. TUNDRA branded into his shoulder an A.

SCORPION: "Cobra?"

TOTEM: "Cobra: so that he will poison. So that he will strangle. So that he will curl around his victims and suffocate them. So that his breath will hypnotize and his eyes will shine in the night, monstrous, golden."

TIGER: "So that he will ooze and blend with the stones. And bite ankles. And with a whack of his sharp scales, strike."

COBRA: "What now?"

TUNDRA: "Nothing."

We took the road back.

The scenery had changed. Through the fog one could see pines, cypresses, and winter plumtrees. We went along a ravine. One of the walls fell vertically, carved, neat like a screen; strains of different sands crossed it—still waves—so polished and shiny that we were reflected in them. The stone corridor echoed our voices, our footsteps on the wet grass, deformed and opaque like the images on the wall.

The opposite slope was not as steep; from its crevices wild olive trees sprouted—*ilex pedunculosa*—whose branches descended to the ground, arborescent peony flowers, lianas and ferns. Among the pebbles dwarf fig trees grew—*ficus pumila*. On the ridge, frost covered a forest of willow trees whose threads, along with those of the frozen water, fell from the summits, cascade of fibers. Among colorless and dry rushes cranes perched; the fluttering of their wings shielded our path. As we advanced the murmur of the water grew louder.

From the highest clefts, skimming the rocks, hemp ropes with baskets tied to their tips were lowered. In those crevices, marked in the cliff by palisades of hay, Buddhist monks lived, naked and alone, mute examiners of the void. The birds knew them and made their nests near-by; hovering around and chirping they guided the few pilgrims, who brought tea and barley meal, to the hampers below the hermits' refuge.

In a corner of the wall *there were several peasant boys who were looking for mushrooms in the grass. They laughed at us, as if surprised at seeing so many strangers in that place.*

We went along a frozen river the hermits always crossed on a blue buffalo when retiring from the world.

Following its winding and ever wider course, covered by white stones, angular and smooth like the vertebrae of prehistoric reptiles, we came upon a meager grotto where the water stopped, crystal-clear; in the white sand at the bottom a dark red grass grew.

The ravine came out onto a misty landscape, of white planes evaporating toward the horizon, where a band of moisture floated over a lake. Milky trunks. Long silvery leaves. Further on, a frail bridge, a small boat. White on white, a bamboo forest. The towers of a monastery.

As we went into the mist we discovered forms, colors appeared. In their burrows—velvety spheres, peaches—startled, ready to roll into a ball, armadillos hid. Among near-by branches, unable to keep their balance, pheasants flew before us, burdened with ornaments, slow in the thickness of the air. Noise among the rushes: it was a fleeing tiger, orange-striped and covered with black marks.

Making our way among the stalks which surrounded us by the thousands, road to the towers, we came upon a stone wall whose junctures were split by bramble-bush. We followed it until we found an opening: a winding road, passing over a bridge in the form of an arch, led to the door of the monastery crowned by a vignette of sealing wax with the inscription "Salut les copains!"

As we opened the door, the face of Buddha appeared before our eyes. His gold colors combined their reflections with those of the green clusters which gave him shade. The steps of a stone staircase and the base of pillars were covered with a moss smooth like cloth. From the back of the great room another staircase began, vertical like a wall, protected by a stone balustrade. This led to a terrace, facing the west: from here we saw an enormous rock more than twenty feet high, in the shape of a loaf of bread. A thin belt of bamboo decorated the base. Continuing to the west and then turning toward the north we went up a slanting corridor leading to the reception room, which consisted of three transoms and faced directly onto the great rock. At the foot of the rock was a fountain in the shape of a half-moon covered by thick bunches of a kind of watercress and fed by water from a spring. The sanctuary, properly speaking, was to the east of the reception room. It was dark and in ruins. A dark green coating, which at certain intervals thickened into yellowish, granular islands with white borders, shrouded the floor. A grey fuzz covered the stone of three of the walls; from the corners, filled with goiters of dark pulp, minute, purple flowers proliferated. Rust signs which seemed sketched in saffron striped the ceiling; drops hanging from these spots lingered a while, and finally fell to the green mold with a dry sound. In the center of the room were the ruins of the altar. The bas-relief of the foundation—a god dancing within a hoop of fire, upon a dwarfish devil; with one of his right hands (a cobra curled around the wrist) the dancer shook a tambourine, with one of his left he raised a torch—it was a nest of mollusks. On the crown mushrooms grew.

A large window sealed by great leaves in the shape of broken circles, like water lilies, filtered a whitish light; beside the window, along the wall, there lay a pond dug into the floor, also carpeted with moss. Swollen white roots were fixed to the bottom, with bony, shiny nodes injected with wine-colored veins.

Joining hands—we could barely walk on the slippery floor —we managed to draw near to the pond. The water was muddy, and in the shadow of the roots, duplicated by the reflection, ivory though deformed symmetries, lethargic and bulbous like the roots, slow fish traveled in a vegetal slumber, wrapped in jelly-like veils, in a tangle of fibers. They let themselves be touched. They did not flee.

We were leaving when TIGER slipped headlong into the pond. He banged the bottom with open hands. Slow, flat, lance-olated animals, open symmetrical leaves with tenuous nerves, hurry back and forth. Streaked with mercury. Mayan faces. Their glowing orange flagelli followed, entangled them.

We helped him up.

It was then that at the door, as if popped by a spring, a monk of the red hat sect appeared: "Do you want me to say a word, a syllable"—he threatened, with clenched fists, frowning —"and turn you into a bird? Do you want me to conjure up five thousand minor demons right this minute, to prick you, to poison your precious body fluids?"

"Make me a gin and tonic"—TIGER answered.

EAT FLOWERS!

I

Petals, filaments (Left foot over the right thigh.): the body is inscribed in a net. (Right foot over the left thigh.) Six flowers mark the middle line. (I cross my arms behind my back.) From the flowers and in all directions forking, interweaving threads branch outward. (I grasp my left heel with the right hand; my right heel with the left.) The man is opaque; the skein is golden. (I lower my head; chin against my chest.) A dark orle, a continuous black line borders the figure, which glowing fibers cross. Every one of his gestures, no matter how sudden or slight, reverberates in the entire texture, like the fright of a fish in its flagelli.

Wrapping myself around myself—ball of yarn, vulva—elbows against my stomach.

The room is white.

Black objects rush toward the walls, attracted by an external gravity.

The floor slopes.

The walls dilate.

The body, motionless, falls.

I was in a creaking enclosure, built upon rushes, over a cliff. It was raining. Below, among the rocks, a wooden building stood in darkness, at ground level, and beyond, a quiet river, meandering among feeble structures resembling fishermen's huts, burrowed a valley. Ribbons of foam crowned the rocks. At sea level and toward the woods, symmetrical paths became blurred as the vegetation, meager and scarce on the banks, thickened; later on the paths reappeared, sinuous, pursued by mule-drivers, bordering slopes and peaks. At certain distances, successive waterfalls cleaved the landscape vertically, just like the grain of the paper does to the surface which unfolds from a roll.

Next to my cell's window, obstructed by a few chopped tree trunks, three enormous nests made of voluminous fibers hung from dry lianas.

On the other slope, less rocky and inclined, enveloped by several layers of humidity, ribbons of varying whites, one could see a pine forest.

Along with the sound of rain, I heard in the distance a constant, grave murmur, the uniform repetition of a single syllable; I heard the unceasing rotation of prayer mills, rattling of flustered children.

Bull aboard
a small boat

down river
across the rain of night.

The room is charred.

White objects come toward the center, toward the exact crossing of its diagonals, and there they remain suspended.

I bring my head down to my knees.

I slowly revolve upon myself.

Within a rolling barrel.

Sitting on a giant peacock—the bird's open tail formed a third halo, behind the red one which surrounded the triple head, and the amber one in which his entire body was inserted—a yellow god appeared. His middle face was calm; on the lateral ones, protruding fangs, irritated and globular eyes, noses fuming smoke. The middle hands together in prayer; the others brandished darts and daggers, bows and arrows. A vertical forefinger pointed toward heaven.

His opal jewels, the settings of which were repeated from the crown to the wide armlets and from there to the bracelets and rings, filled the room with an orange radiance.

On a wicker arm-chair, attracted, lethargized by that light, in slow flight a pheasant came to perch.

The king smiles, displays his weapons.

The peacock's claws, streaked with chalk, hold fast to the sand; the bird raises its sharp, ebony head.

The room is white / is charred / is white.

Wrapping myself around myself, elbows against my stomach. I await—has it happened already?—the crash, the white blackout, blindness, a second grasped only by the languor of memory.

Thick glass, sand falling, cracking clay.

Silence. Headlights in the distance.

Yellow plain that is crossed by the runway.

Discontinuous, a stripe vanishes into the horizon.

Arrows. The wind sketches and erases terraces upon the sand, strokes that go back and forth; breaches appear on the edges, darker palisades, sparking walls that wind like snakes. That stiff swelling wave—shrouded dunes, shuffled planes— covers the highway, blackens the gigantic yellow arrows which curve to the right and signal the name of a city—we walk over the letters—a cipher.

Wrapping myself around myself.

On this side of the fractures, on this side of the grooved screen, the body, motionless, falls.

SCORPION: He shakes his lion's mane, breaks a golden Tibetan necklace, takes out his phallus and pisses: "We had danced till dawn, they'd made us go round and round—the music just wouldn't stop, the hoarse howlers—; already we were drinking out of mugs without handles, the ones you hold with open hands, we were covered with the beads the musicians gave us and were smoking with them, too. Only then did we discover what their instruments were: the flutes: hollowed skin-bones; the loose, rotten teeth that hung in their alveoli resounded in their skulls; the skin that covered the drums was tattooed—blue dots—with eagles. Deathly party: we were dancing with the ugliest girl."

The shaved heads laughed, ran away—we lammed into them—their bones still resounding. Orange cloaks floated like flags.

I trampled on the instruments. Spat on them. I kicked holes into the skulls of the tambourines, went crazy on top of them and threw to the floor the funeral amulets in which, surrounded by amber beads, protected by two pieces of cut glass, little porous bones were heaped—baby teeth, bird cartilage—; I sprayed them with my cum.

A metal disk was left among the broken apophyses, a snail-shell among thorns; with his crest he flattened jingle bells, bone splinters.

TOTEM: "We masturbated: TIGER and TUNDRA; SCORPION and I. Each one came alone. Nobody touched the other guy's cum. We didn't look at each other."

TIGER: "It's snowing. I tell you it's snowing"—the first flakes fall immediately.

Like aluminum, in the distance, the lakes. Covered bridges go over them. On the shores, austere fortress towers, cedar palaces, tall dovecotes amidst cherry orchards, ruins of synagogues, truncated minarets.

"It's so cold in this country that not even the tea spills over!"

Checkered, identical compartments go by, regularly lighted by neon tubes, skyscrapers are separated by frozen canals, treeless avenues, aerial rails, superimposed turnpike loops.

On a magazine cover, TUNDRA appears on a motorscooter, seated like a yogi. The white smoke that comes out of the exhaust pipe forms a third halo behind the red one—a spotlight—which surrounds the head, and behind the silver halo—aluminum cylinders—in which his entire, nude body is inserted.

TO SCORPION

Afterwards, we shall read your bones.

With a burning metal rod we shall touch each shoulder-blade:

on the fractures, omens.

With black ink

we shall write messages to your descendants on your skeleton,

your engraved frame will serve as our herald:

ciphers, dates, whom we were,
the age that befell us to live in.
Afterwards, we shall protect everything with lacquer.

TO TOTEM

Not the empty nets
but rather the support of all forms:
you wanted love—the dissolution—
the Diamond's body.

You didn't know what you were asking for,
what ceremony you entered:
you invoked, you demanded
—the masters tried to discourage you—
you stopped drinking and eating
until, naturally, something possessed you.
You had convulsions,
you rolled on the floor, as if overcome by some poison;
bundle of discordant gestures, your body was escaping you,
you did somersaults,
you played a sitar that nobody saw.

What were you dancing?
Whom were you addressing,
disjointed pantomime, dispersed gestures?
What demon did you embody in an aphasic opera?

You were impervious to pain, to human presence.
You crawled over red hot steel sheets.
You slashed your skin with them,
and then,
lest you would ever repeat what you had seen,

you cut your own tongue from its root,
and threw it, in a stream of blood, among burning coals.
The ashes were gathered.
With petal ashes and honey we drank them.

Now,
dumb and mute,
in your limbo
—love is intolerable—
they keep you in a sanctuary, monster of public concern,
amidst incense burners, prayer mills,
red porcelain bull-dogs and great golden gongs
which the servants pound as you pass.

Fed daily with wild doves
—fed daily with butterflies—
bathed and dried daily
upon ladders according to their rank
the thousand prescribed snakes
which defend your abode
sleep in the whorls of altars
in the moldings of furniture
in drawers and in ritual cups,
and nest in your sleeves and hats
—at night you can hear them curling into knots,
searching for the moisture of the trees—.

There will you remain until your death
among statues and stupas
—God is intolerable—.
Until your death is paid by the State
—perhaps love is that—.
Taxes must be good for something.

TO TIGER

In the autumn you would come out of the forest
of the western highland
and raze the plain
—the constellations of the quadrant
rose in the night sky—.
You were white.
You had firm legs, excellent thighs,
that looked like elephant trunks; similar
and fleshy were
your knees.
You possessed all the signs:
your thick eyebrows were joined, and between them,
scarred, a circle.
You displayed the cranial protuberance.
Your neck was marked by three creases,
like a snail-shell:
When I saw you, I knew you were a god.

Like stars, men rise and fall.
Your guards will be of no use
of no use your flying horses.
All yin comes out in winter.
You can invoke.
You can conjure.
You will burn.

TO TUNDRA

Draw on your chest the dragons fighting.
Take care in your performance.
Watch out for the details.
Do not use either a hog's bristle brush

nor one of rabbit hair;
try the softest: mouse whiskers or children's hair.
The flaming heads will form a face:
The crests of the monsters will sketch the eyebrows,
the claws a smiling mouth.
Do not rush.
Do not squander.
Use black ink as though it were gold.
Invoke upon awakening.
Meditate each line.
Because you will see death with those very eyes.
After the report of gunfire: dirt in your eyes.
Headlights turned on at midday.

The air of hospitals,
of the dying and of white robes.
Of one who among forceps and red cotton,
pustules and screams
headbands and shrouds
stagnates, dense: I breathe.

On a green table, as narrow as a scaffold, head reclined on
a stake, a gaping and toothless young man lay, his abdomen
empty, his eyes swollen, small spheres divided by black grooves.

Next to the stretched body stood four girls equally grey
and combed, wearing enormous lace hats punctuated by yellow
flowers. One of them had folded down the wide brim of her
hat—only her mouth could be seen; another had turned hers
up and showed her face, proudly.

A chubby one, smaller than the previous two, holding on to
a blue muslin embroidered with scales from a discarded snake-
skin, was opening her mouth under her disproportionate pink
algae hat, resting her chin on an open hand, and her elbow on
the body.

Another girl was coming out of the basement. She was not covered by a hat, but rather, of course, by an open umbrella.

Useless are the skills of dissection,
the formaldehyded gloves,
the cough of the coroners,
the cotton balls in the mouth.
Useless are the exact pins of the shroud.
Cartesian, the dead always remain
looking
at their feet.

Our traveling companions were Mongols from the kingdom of Khartchin, who were repairing in pilgrimage to the Eternal Sanctuary; and who had with them their Grand Chaberon; that is to say, a Living Buddha, the superior of their Lamasery. The Chaberon was a young man of eighteen, whose manners were agreeable and gentlemanly, and whose face, full of ingenious candor, contrasted singularly with the part which he was constrained to enact. At the age of five he had been declared Buddha and Grand Lama of the Buddhists of Khartchin, and he was now about to pass a few years in one of the Grand Lamaseries of Lha-Ssa, in the study of prayers and of the other knowledge befitting his dignity. A brother of the King of Khartchin and several Lamas of quality were in attendance to escort and wait upon him.

. . . after following for several days a long series of valleys in which, at certain distances, black tents and great herds of buffaloes appeared, at last we camped near a great Tibetan village.

. . . it was not, however, a village properly speaking, but rather, one of several ample farms well-finished in terrazo, finely painted with whitewash. These were surrounded by great trees and crowned by a small tower in the shape of a dovecote where

flags, of all colors and covered with Tibetan sentences, floated.

. . . shortly before arriving at the base of the mountain, the whole caravan halted on a level spot where there stood an Obo, or Buddhic monument, built with piled stones, surmounted by flags and bones covered with inscriptions.

. . . we bent over the edge of the plateau and saw beneath us an immense glacier jutting out tremendously, and bordered with frightful precipices. We could distinguish, under the light coating of snow, the greenish hue of ice. We took a stone from the Buddhic monument and threw it down the glacier. A loud noise was heard, and the stone, gliding down rapidly, left after it a broad green line.

. . . the flames were consuming the dry grass in their path with such fearful speed that they soon reached our camels. Their long thick manes were burning. We ran to them armed with our felt carpets, endeavoring to smother the flaming bodies.

Men and birds have their place here (I imagine concentric squares); stars and their orbits, the snows, blind stones, and those that support a temple, everything here will come to contemplate its own identity, everything will climb to its own center. (Those black lines support my thought, its diagram structures and clarifies it, it does not escape from that framework.) From the outside inward surge rivers, clouds, assemblies of demons, flights of the chosen, their enormous footprints and from the circle inserted in his forehead, between the joined eyebrows, the glow.

Surrounded by trees, white (In that blueprint I search for my body's own.) houses begin to appear in the inside squares; the cities are isolated, as on a map (web within another web). From Mount Meru, everything emanates, expansion of the void, succession of syllables (I repeat the syllable.), compact, firm, earthy double of the dark emblem, snowy on its peak, in one piece, pineapple thrust, stone, stupa, Buddha.

I was alone, in a carpeted apartment, with white walls and furniture. Sitting on the floor (outside it snowed) my legs folded like a yogi, naked.

On the wall an Albers.

II

The faithful are sitting under the great foot, doing their thing, as one would say. The smell of urine, among other smells—a poster of "The Wild One": the bubble coming out of its mouth says MEN—detectable under that of hash, and take a good sniff, of the filth typical of taverns in the Malay archipelago, doesn't bother them.

A green neon light curves to form the heel, sketches the toe sinuously, the arch of the foot with a continuous line; the shadow of the sole is in chalk.

Through changing screens of uselessly mentholated smoke one can see, holding tight to their machines, pinball players; behind, a naked man tied to a post—the door to WOMEN.

The walls: blow-ups of women in transparent kimonos, racing cars, a Nepalese temple, Karel Appel, Che Guevara. Flowers.

Between records—the very same that's dropping under the needle—one can hear the rattling of the machines, thrusts against the wall; light bulbs flicker on the backboards; strawberries, clubs, lemons, cherries fall.

Without an electric eye and without anybody pushing it, the small peeling door to the Rembrandtsplein opens heavily, slowly: the guru has come.

"My head"—he declaims, adding one more gesture to those five ritual gestures with which he made his entrance, while the players fuss over the machines—"is a perfect oval, my eyes have the shape of lotus petals, my lips have the fullness of the mango and the arch of my eyebrows is an imitation of Krishna's. Fix me a tableful of rice. And, I beg you PLEASE, don't touch me"—he holds off the curious with a hand reeking of incense and the faithful with a shove. "Ask your questions from afar. Every man for himself. I care little for the human race. And enough sighs, please. I travel by jet, *not* by elephant. Holiness is so boring."

The Most High One takes off his orange hat, the rings—fake tiger teeth—he wears on each finger. He drops onto a bench, under the great neon foot, among torn cushions, knapsacks and shoes. In the dust cloud that rises, some longhairs grunt, startled, and push him; they turn around and go back to sleep. The Master pulls off his shoes—sandals in spite of the below zero weather, scatters glass beads and tin rings. He chooses one of his kerchiefs for the night, and one of his blondest followers for lover. Hand in hand they cross the smoke screens, the rows of players, the barely opened door of MEN. The mustard-colored light reveals scribbled walls and two urinals ditched with thick, opalescent water. The guru touches his forehead: "You have been chosen from all the rest," he whispers in his ear; he fondles his navel and kisses it. The blond boy, erect, soon reaches ecstasy: "I am about to enter the isles of the blessed," and he grabs the sink faucet. "I can already see the Heaven of the West!"

Before the peeling mirror the Supreme One shoots up.

He comes back from the toilet most cryptic.

"I have not subverted anybody," he grumbles, eyes ablaze. "What a smell of burnt grass! Verily I say unto you that truth can be anything, that a true god cannot be distinguished from a mad-man or comedian. Let's have more ice. And would you please stop that music. Barbarism, your name is the Western World."

SCORPION: "What should I do to get rid of the reincarnation cycle?"

THE GURU: "Learn to breathe."

(Applause. Laughter. Silence.) (An Abyssinian athlete faints.) (Four nude pin-ups, smeared with Ambre Solaire, slip in through a half-opened window, forefingers on their lips and carrying overnight bags. Coup de théâtre: as they reach the center of the room they draw out of their bags four newly starched Salvation Army uniforms and four giant money boxes. Buttoned from head to toe in a white coif, they shake the collection tray, starting with the guru and toward the four cardinal points: fracas of florins.)

TOTEM: "What's the best spiritual exercise?"

THE GURU: "Sit down. Place your left foot over the right thigh and the right over the left. Cross your arms behind your back. Grab your left heel with your right hand; the right heel with your left. Look at your navel. And then try to unravel . . ."

(A young Moroccan—pitch black body, smooth and shiny, grape-colored pupils—dances to the rhythm of the numismatic quartet. A Dutchman bathes the boy's head, thick Karakul tapestry, in dark beer which runs down his back and between his buttocks.) (Out of a chewing-gum machine, Don Luis de Góngora emerges:

"Foam down his back:
on the ebony frost!"

TIGER: "What's the quickest way to liberation?"

THE GURU: "Don't think about it."

(Sighs. Interjections of approval.) (Shirley Temple comes out of the men's room.) (The narcotics squad comes in: polyurethane muskets, shields of expanded epoxy.) (A black man takes the backboard off a pinball machine: hides a kif ball in each light-bulb and a syringe in the groove for the aluminum balls. Another black hides a diamond in the inside pump of the toilet and then swallows a list of Buddhist maxims, another one containing the names of the members of the Supreme Soviet— which he had previously copied in white ink, although translated into Swahili, upon the folds of his testicles—and still another, in color, containing top secret designs of the new winter fashions.)

TUNDRA: "What formula should I repeat so as not to be reincarnated as a pig?"

THE GURU:

Ubiquitous is the whiteness of heavenly purity and happiness; ubiquitous are the snowy, shadowless, immutable bodies of the divine. The silence and the unique gesture of zero are perfect.

Marine, invisible, forever blue, are the demi-gods that surround us, the weightless ones.

Neither word nor object, in his own yellow world of successive circles man is moving.

I suffer in it. Sunken under my feet are antelopes of grass, sparrows of sweet basil, snakes of mint, animals and birds.

What a commotion the elves cause against the red walls!

O Humanity, what demons and what a blackness befalls you, as night does, upon the plain.

He finished the prayer frantically scratching his head.

"Religion, my dears"—he added psalmodically—"is sound."

And he shook a small bell. From the back of the room one of the faithfuls answered him with a small bone flute.

"What a life!" he sighed. "I must travel east for the spring equinox, south for the summer solstice, to the heart of the west when fall arrives and to the far north in the dead of winter! I'm going then," and the peeling door opens by itself again. Before passing through it, the Unique One turns to the distracted crowd for the last time and states:

I RECOMMEND THE INGESTION OF PETALS

FOR THE BIRDS

I

"O nobly-born, COBRA,
the time has come for you to seek the Path.
Your breathing is about to cease.
Your instructor has set you face to face to the Clear Light;
and now you are about to experience it:
heaven empty things,
clear intelligence,
transparent void
without circumference or center.

Know thyself;
Lucidly.
I take you to the test."

BARDO THÖDOL.

With Cobra's body over his shoulders—the perforated head bleeds from the nose, against the nape of his neck, on his right shoulder—here comes TOTEM; on his coat, down the leg of his pants, to the cuffs, two scarlet stripes: cadet in his Sunday best.

He shines phosphorescently: mint drivel, the dead man's green drool bathes him; a cloying cloak of concentric humors covers him. Hunched over, he presses onward: wooden Dutch beggar, hunter bent under the excessive gifts of hunting; what he carries is not a corpse, but coppery ducks instead, guts with holes and flaccid necks; pelleted swans, claws, feathers.

They sound like nuts cracking, but actually he's stepping on blind crabs who are desperately fleeing from the smell of death.

More daring still are the birds, who are pecking at the two heads, savoring the ganglia cocktail.

THE BIRDS' COURSE

They pierce cellophane packages—dehydrated potato chips —on the tables of restaurant terraces, they take flight—concentric circles, the wider, the slower—they perch on corpses abandoned on nearby towers, they play, fight, eat, defecate over them; they take flight again—a spiral accelerating as it closes— spitting cartilage and toe-nails, teeth and hair over the conical roofs of temples, over trolleycars, into pools and courtyards, into barges filled with folly and the holy—long black hair, white tunics—with fakers and gods; the birds, pecking at eyes, vomiting bone-marrow, off to the terraces once more, chirping, without mistakes, without faults, guided by the river, by coal dusts, by the grey stains of ashes and by fistfuls of red petals scattered to the air; the birds, spitting skin over the steps that go down to the stinking water where children play among yellow-turbaned cachetic impostors.

TIGER, TUNDRA, and SCORPION had fled.

COBRA always had a liking for cheap shows: TOTEM recalled the initiation, the tin frog, the yogurt and the ketchup; so he entered the morgue howling, between showy fainting spells, drowning in saffron tears which he dried with his mournful cravat.

The night watchman was a faded and shaky Indonesian who held a small camphor bag in his fist. Before him and with effective vaudeville gestures, the mourner displayed his consternation.

They had already stored him in the cellar.

They went down a crippled and smelly staircase. Through scaffolds and rope-wheels, under a light-shaft soiled by pigeons, black ropes, strung from the highest supports at determined intervals, secured stairsteps, fastened beams, held wedges firm.

A greasy, sweetish odor rose from the lower chambers: "The sponge of intestines, opening"—explained the Asiatic custodian touching the tip of his nose while making a disgusted little face.

He recognized him among the repeated dissected bodies, in the blinking of an acetylene light—according to their custom, in a pool of formaldehyde, the drowned were spinning, adrift. He was still warm.

Posthumous homage: a friendly neighborhood theater effect: out of his pocket he pulled a dagger of gross dimensions, its sinuous blade engraved with the eight emblems of good fortune, and taking advantage of a yawn, he buried it to the handle in the watchman's mouth.

He fled with the body over his shoulders. The crushed head bled from the nose, against the nape of his neck, on his right shoulder.

He fled with a rainbow background of a mountain and seven circles of oceans separated by seven circles of golden hills.

He fled with a harbor background.

With a rainbow background of a mountain and seven circles of oceans separated by seven circles of golden hills.

On its peak, just opened, foamy and snowy, a bottle; two glasses with ice; lemon peels hanging on the rims.

With a harbor background: in the forefront buoys and masts were piled, Shell's wooden fences—a heart bordered by a thin red neon tube—empty spheres, of green glass, a giant tube, of tin, ejecting a white cylinder with fluorescent stripes. Motionless seagulls. Hard flags.

Behind, and on the other side of the estuary, of the coal barges, a grey plain of grass spread out, squared off by the shiny lines of the canals; at certain distances, in the rectangular gardens bordered by the water, lamaist funeral piles rose, their golden white-striped needles pointing to the clouds. Distant red ochre. Upon the rooftops old cypress trees cast their shadows.

Further away, on the horizon, a windmill.

He shook his head. He came to. He was looking at a collage posted on the MEN's door—clippings from LIFE—in a shabby and weedy café in Rembrandt plaza.

He came in the kitchen door. He wiped the dining table with a rag dripping lye. He lay the corpse down. He covered it with a tablecloth.

Over the four straight, nickel-plated cylinders, in the middle of the black bakelite sheet, shrouded to his mouth in oil cloth, COBRA was getting cold; his nose dripped into the silverware drawer.

"Don't anyone look at him," TOTEM ordered the first trembling arrivals. "Don't anyone say his name. Don't anyone touch his feet or he'll go straight to hell. Build a paper effigy with lots of arms around the trunk, like the spokes of a wheel. Paint an eye on each hand. Hang it up like a lamp over a table. Silence.

Tell his instructor. Tell the people at Rembrandt's to come over, but let each bring his own food."

TIGER appeared: barefoot, shaven skull; wrapped in a yellow sheet, a red bonnet in his hand:

"Everybody out." —The new scabbed arrivals protested. The lama pushed them into the living room and slammed the door. He bolted the back screen door, closed the wickets which faced onto the canal, onto a row of brick façades with very high windows and, still further away, onto a bridge.

He drank from the faucet. With the back of his hand he dried his mouth. He rolled a mat; he sat next to the dead man. He whispered something in his ear, then, parting his hair, examined the skull: he tore a lock out of the parietal joint.

He talked to him for an hour.

Running circles around the corpse—he stuck the head to the knees, heels to the buttocks—starting with the feet, he wrapped him in adhesive tape, girdling him, an innocent in glass clay.

Between the white bands, on his thighs, there remained fine watery adhesions, parallel spindles which were breaking off: a red seam, like an eyebrow; under the transparent skin, minute, black, capillar flowers burst open.

Thus wrapped—embryo and mummy—he left him in a corner, leaning against the refrigerator and contemplating an electric dishwasher.

For four days they received seedy condolences and fed the libbers from Rembrandtsplein. They would run, between Tibetan sighs, to the automat on the corner. They would bring back cold cuts, vegetable salad in boxes, apple turnovers and even dwarf mangoes imported from China.

Among butter lamps, conch shells and flageolets, tiny petal cups and five unfinished or worm-eaten statues—a portly Buddha pointing to the ground—there piled fruit peels, fluorescent teaspoons, paper plates smeared with rancid mayonnaise, flower-printed napkins and thermos cups which they passed around—hash brownies—from hand to hand.

While they officiated in the kitchen, TUNDRA and SCORPION took turns cleaning, and preparing the food which, in a big cup, the Instructor presented to the dead man and then renewed, once the subtle, invisible essence was extracted.

The mourners dozed off, stacked in corners, under faded or ragged banners of prayers, among books nobody knew how to read any longer, nor which could be preserved in a stupa, tambourines—yak-skin stretched over skull halves—amulets and mandalas. They cuddled up against discarded statues—cleared by antique dealers, auctioned as premium along with cargoes of Burgundian madonnas, Chichimec heads or copies of Murillo's "Ascension"—whose piety or anger had not been restored by the faith and constant offerings of the four lamas, far, as they were, from the pristine sources; crossed legs and lotus flowers served as pillows to the filthy; to those lacking an earlobe or the cranial protuberance, thrones of Buddhas, or to those who had sawed off the tuft, or stolen the paste of glass eyes, or yielded to the perseverance of termites.

Drinking down Nescafé and cough pills, eating and pissing, the wailers spent the day in the shade, their eyes opaque, talking to themselves, far gone, exchanging, with lifeless gestures, wooden tablets they spent hours examining: in concentric circles of all colors, narrow-waisted and big-assed women, wrapped in red garments and flying—their black hair floats, from the same spiral as the clouds—thousands of pilgrims, titans and demons, palaces, rivers. In the center, a mountain.

On the fourth day, the knowledge factor abandoned COBRA's body.

Newly bathed and smelling of Maja, TOTEM, giving jocular slaps, went among the raving harlequins.

He uttered a rotund "That's all folks" which rendered the dinner guests compunctious and disgusted.

TIGER checked the corners of the mouth and the eyelids, the orifices of the nose and the ears, of the penis and anus: they secreted a yellow sap, a thick and purulent humor.

With a chair and his clothes, he began to assemble the dead man's image. He slid pants on the front legs as well as a pair of boots; he dressed the back with a red sweater, he buckled a worn-out and dirty antelope jacket: on the back one could still see a vertical arch opened in the hide, dripping, soaked in by the plush, writhing like a mangled snake; then, like yesteryear, sketched in a single stroke by an expert penman with an angular style, the circle of Divination, twisted over itself and edgeless, the perfect hoop; stamped by a stone seal, beside the circle a square mark: BR; branded into the shoulder, an A.

On the neck he stuck a printed sheet of paper that revealed holes and threads when held up to the light; in the center, the figure of the deceased with his legs girdled, praying over a lotus flower and surrounded by things most pleasing to the senses:

mirror
conch-shell and lyre
flower pot
pastries in a chalice
silk dresses, a canopy.

Beside the left shoulder, vertical arabesque, six phonetic symbols:

god
titan
man
beast
unhappy spirit
hell.

On the bottom, a prayer:
"I, who depart from this world"—here they sketched his

name: TUNDRA the arch and the circle, SCORPION the monogram and final A—"COBRA, worship and take refuge in my lama director and in all the deities, both peaceful and wrathful.

"May the Great Pious One forgive all the sins I have accumulated and all the impurities of my former lives and may He lead me on the road to another good world."

TOTEM brought a black scarf, of fine wool, which the deceased himself had stolen from a drugstore; TIGER tied one of the ends to his neck.

"Eat what you want," he whispered to him, "from what we have given you. But bear in mind that you are dead, so don't come back to this house any more and don't start bothering the living. Remember my name, and with that help take the straight road, the white road. Right this way . . ."

He pulled the other end of the scarf, and began to lead the funeral procession while chanting a liturgy and jingling a bell. He was followed by TUNDRA, blowing into a sea-shell and by SCORPION, with cymbals which he banged against COBRA's body from time to time. In his left hand TOTEM carried a tambourine: he'd flip it over and a few metal balls hanging from ribbons would beat against the skin; TIGER himself, interrupting the liturgy, played a femur-flute.

Every once in a while the lama director would turn around to invite the dead man's spirit to join its body and to assure him that the route they were following was the right one. Behind him came the pall-bearers with the corpse and, along with candy and sodas, the rest of the grimy riff-raff. The ragged wiped their eyes, howling sporadically, sobbing between puffs of smoke.

When the funeral ended, the paper face was burned.

By the color of the flames and their manner of burning, they knew the departed was on the right road.

"With a derisive support," TUNDRA congratulated himself, "I have succeeded in visualizing the dead man's insides."

SCORPION, who had been examining a mandala for some time, abandoned his rigorous contemplation in order to listen to him.

"Yes"—the enlightened one added—"by these stains on the wall I have known it: black grass grows in COBRA's intestines! Want me to trace his curriculum mortis for you? Very well, at this moment he is contemplating the fifty-eight divinities, irritated hoarders of Knowledge, inserted in concentric hoops of fire. Wrathful and blood-sucking flames surround him. Four disheveled black demons make faces at him while they devour small bodies in large chunks. Surrounding these large-fanged monsters, beasts with pelican and frog heads, drooling blood and ganglia, scream upon a dark rainbow."

But, so many drawings had to have some use! The late-lamented knows: that hair-raising Cinerama is purely an emanation from the lower part of his brain.

The wheel will break.

He will reach safe harbor.

From the paper face
they gathered the ashes on a platter.

They mixed them with clay.

With that paste they modeled minute relics, letters and symbols.

They offered a few upon the altar of the house,
others, beneath trees and protruding rocks,
upon hills and cross-roads.

While they burned the page they undressed the chair.

They auctioned off the clothes among the ragpickers.

"With these florins"—TOTEM warned, "we shall throw a party in his honor . . . in a year's time."

ANATOMY LESSON

You were diagonal, yellowing. You were a dead weight, a perfect, knotless wooden pole, a found object which the curious four examined.

They read you. Pointed at you. Confronted your body with a sketched body—a map of Man, opened—; they enumerated your parts, named your viscera, opened your eyelids—dimmed globes—taking notes, they turned the page.

Next to your calloused feet impregnated with brimstone, there was a book, unfolded like a musical score.

They sank their fingertips into your flesh: the imprints of the tips, the grooves of the nails, remained: you were made of wax, of paper, of soft marble, of clay.

They slashed your wrists with a scalpel; they tightened bindings around your arm, starting at the shoulder. From the wound gushed a black paste which they collected in a small case. In two others they kept samples of your urine and excrement.

Those three residues, dissolved in urine, sprayed the funeral banquet.

They wanted to throw him into a canal wrapped in a fiery-colored cloak so that once the water froze he would remain on the sandy bottom, the soles of his feet facing up, cloak opened, and the children would point at him beneath their ice skates, trapped in the glass;

they wanted to cremate him: ashes within a cobra of carved scales—its eyes two coarse emeralds, its tongue a ruby zig-zag—whose head uncurled;

they wanted to embalm him, seated and holding a swastika, to preserve him in the basement, surrounded by daggers with emblems and dried oranges.

Finally, a lama astrologer calculated the horoscope of death: at six o'clock they had to take him up to the hills.

They cut his skin into strips which they nailed to the rocks.
They crushed his bones.

They mixed this dust with barley flour. They scattered it to the wind.

They repeated the syllables for the last time.

They abandoned everything.
For the birds.

II

In hollow heads of benevolent Buddhas the five transformers received the coke balls which they'd extract by unscrewing pupils and then refine. The ninth sublimation would turn the curds into their white and light opposites. A resentful and irascible addict delivered the statues masqueraded as a diligent antiquarian and effeminate Tibetologist. He had given them this warehouse where several traders in Asian art accumulated their fraudulent junk in its front rooms.

They wrapped the distilled snow in small jute sacks—scent bags!—in thin packages without depth, adjustable to shoe soles; they hid it in small circular boxes of TJING LJANG YU, essential balm—with a sky-blue background, in relief, a turquoise pagoda of conical roofs: The Temple of Heaven—they concealed it in inflated condom balloons, they dyed it, red sugar.

All day long in artful, frantic enterprise, inflamed, feverish, poisoned by their own waste, infected by their own refuse: thus the fanatics survived.

They had deserted the too hot and crowded upstairs rooms of the warehouse; the refiner was at work in the condemned cellar which the stench of the nearby canal invaded. Outside and next to the counterfeit windows which yesteryear had been covered with thick stained-glass, from whose frames broken circles, dismounted shields and twisted iron flowers still survived, there accumulated—blankets of foam dragged by the drainage of the Garden's Indonesian laundries—scattered oil stains with spread-winged dead ducks floating on top of them; stale food, pecked at by the birds, fermented among pine-wood and empty tin cans.

From the deepest rooms—a labyrinth of crumbled steps, irregular doors, and humid hallways on the other side of which one could sense the ditched water—the traders of white no longer emerged except to deliver the little bags and boxes among the sweet-toothed and punctual Rembrandtsplein "connections"; they'd choke themselves with smoked sardines on top of piled apple crates, they'd urinate hurriedly and in dark corners; seeking the delicate metamorphoses, sampling finer and finer sand, they'd drink sugar water, sleep sitting up.

To maintain themselves in that fever they would consume the product of their own gestures: on domestic trips they'd burn the most subtle part of their craftsmanship, the swiftest jewels, the neatest grooves.

They sank further and further; to deepen the dungeon, they'd dump rubbish into the canal, they advanced into the most humid places, perforated walls, dug the ground—the light became a pin-cushion and a sea-urchin; moles digging holes.

They slept wrapped in straw mats. Ears against the wall, they listened from the other side of their sleep to the sluggish flow of the water on the bed of the canal, its filtering between the stones, the dripping from the eaves over the thick oily sheet, slowly undulating on the surface, the festering of the sewers.

Once a week they had to abandon the coolness.

They ascended. Well into the night, they'd emerge, suffocated by heat and fear. In the crypt they'd armor themselves with small bags and metal boxes.

More congested and tinkling than a leaping dwarf wearing a vest of coins, COBRA climbed a column around which there still were remains of steps, hanging on like propellers. He'd raise a hatchway, inspect the warehouse through the crack, fling it wide open, whistle intermittently like a blind owl. Scarily looking everywhere at once, the four remaining heads, wrinkled and dark, began cropping up, one by one, on the white floor tiles. The hairy eyebrows turned right and left: their locks swept the tiles. When a bearded sphere, a giggle, would rise, the one below pushed up like a spring: on the lime background, among the depot's broken down statues, the fugitive distillers suddenly appeared: glazed carnivalesque demons, large oval eyes of transparent indigo, automatons from a cathedral clock striking five.

Behind the guide, tinted by the oblique veins of the earth, panting and layered turrets, TOTEM, TIGER and TUNDRA appeared. They gave another signal, a foot stamping on the hatchway, a scream: SCORPION germinated.

The five of them now in exile, they closed the entrance to the refined inferno, to Proserpine's underground estate. In single file, crocked, brimming with creaking paper wrappers, coated like glazed pineapples by a thin sugary layer, winter doves covered in snow, they crossed the nave.

Far off, they listened to the squeak of trolleycars, footsteps in the street, their metallic, empty repetition refracted by the naves, voices in summer's splendor—volumes, vessels—their muted reflection against the wooden gods.

Piling up on either side and, at some spots, even up to the concrete ceiling, the spiteful ancients: a smiling Maitreya displayed the hind-side of its unscrewed eyeballs: the convexity of the globes, both irises painted, fell from the hinge of the lower eyelids, like the open cover of a clock.

An Avalokitesvara mercifully showed the palm of his right hand supplied with a pupil: one of his own unscrewed ears was hanging from a forefinger; a blackish cornea, like the one in a magpie's beak, lined the inside of the skull-case. At certain intervals, on the petals of a jointed throne in the shape of a lotus flower—the prince lay face down—as if someone with a scissors' tip had torn off big lumps of the same dark rind —below, over red sealing wax, small sheets of gilt; the opaque crust, the nail pickings that clog bronchial tubes and drain pipes, had taken over everything, even the rear end of the dismounted statue.

All that remained among the displaced venerables were the intruders, who, though demolished, were worthy, worn down either by the sea or devout lips, their features faded—how pious hands rub!—proud and splintered: their cloaks restored, their hearts intact, the tin of daggers and crowns glittering; all pointed toward the beams on the ceiling, euphoric annunciators, relinquished Sevillian martyrs, worm-eaten mahogany madonnas, pious baroque women of jacaranda, contracted monks and fatuous archangels.

In order to pass between a solar quadrant and a player piano, a Flemish peasant lightly lifts his right foot and picks up his cloak to his knees; his hair and beard of identical whorls—gothic flowers of cauliflower—fall to his waist. Straddling his shoulders, two chubby little legs fall in front of his chest, the small feet among the beard's snail shells: they are joined to a little boy's trunk and this, in turn, to an arm pierced by termites that raises a golden sphere—cross on the north pole.

On a black rug scanned by a texture of tigers and white letters, a maiden hurls a wheel bristling with barbed wire.

To slide open a metal door, COBRA pushed aside a leprous beggar whose concentric sores were licked by hungry dogs.

They could barely stand the night's glare, the noises reverberated in their heads. There were motorcycles lying on the sidewalk. It was raining. In the square one could hear the distant guitar-strumming of the inns, far off. At the subway entrance a frightened woman appeared. She was wearing a red hat; its ribbons, falling from the brim to her black cape, hid the gold flowers on her face.

They walked against the walls, slipping through the crowd. They wanted to flee, return to the cloister, be someone else. They didn't look or talk to one another: they took different sidewalks, crestfallen.

"The itching rain of glances is making us soaking wet," hummed TOTEM and TIGER *a dúo*.

"Mocking eyes give us the once over. Fingers point at us, put asterisks on us," quoted sweaty TUNDRA.

Same slowness of gestures—they were walking on the bottom of an aquarium; they were floating over the same glass fiber, advancing over the same beard a few millimeters from the floor.

They saw the same colors, one word contained them all. Transparent spheres. An iris haloed things.

The same horizontal and fixed rictus stretched all their lips.

Between records—the very same that's dropping under the needle—one can hear the rattling of the machines, thrusts against the wall; light bulbs flicker on the backboards, strawberries, clubs, lemons, cherries fall.

Without an electric eye and without anybody pushing it, the small peeling door to the Rembrandtsplein opens heavily, slowly: Rosa, the seer, has come.

Her neckline plunges to her navel; a white flower fastens it between her breasts. She doesn't greet anybody—that's Rosa for you—she doesn't return anybody's greeting. A black bead necklace, funerary Baroque showpiece, chokes her throat.

She settles at a purple table, next to the MEN's door. She immediately arranges her deck of cards in an arc. With a filed nail, polished in her very own scarlet, she points to the ace of hearts—a golden cobra curled around her forefinger; with the other hand she's holding the arm of her glasses: a green plastic snake bordering the eyes shapes the frame. She sticks out her tongue, fluted like a U, the most lucid lady, she turns her head: out of her hair, splinters of scorched mahogany, out of the wide-brim hat touching it, a pastel blue fox-tail leaps, its very tip opening near the cards into a tuft of turquoise feathers.

"Ask, gentlemen. About life and death. But remember I am nothing but a concretion of the primeval viscous chloride, a creature of the eternal and full truculence." —She sticks out her tongue again, touches up a beauty mark:—"We must dramatize the uselessness of everything!"—and she breaks into laughter.

People crowd around her. Under the great foot fringed by a fluorescent tube we take advantage of the mob to hand out red boxes. We glue ourselves to the customers from behind. Into pants' pockets we slide our right hand. On the bottom we leave a Temple of Eden. We glue ourselves in front of the customers. On the right, into our pants' pockets, we feel their sliding hands, warm against our thighs. On the bottom, a ticket is left behind.

Near the urinals, under the mustard light of the MEN, shrouded by smoke, by the greenish and lukewarm vapor of urine, the essential balm is propagated in circular cases which we tear from our bodies—poisoned talismans—; snow is scattered among black ideograms.

We distract the cardsharp:

SCORPION: What should I do in order to have a chest like Superman's?
ROSA: Learn to breathe.

Stuck to a convex base, a skull with frightened eyes looks up, imploringly, and shows a reddened tongue, opened in a U, like Rosa's. Over the skull—its claw scratches the bone—a stuffed crow displays a daisy beaded on a necklace.

COBRA: I'd like to be an acrobat in the *Palace of Wonders*. What should I do to loosen up my joints?
ROSA: Sit down. Place your left foot over the right thigh and the right over the left. Cross your arms behind your back. Grab your left heel with your right hand; the right heel with your left. Look at your navel. And then try to unravel . . .

Behind the card dealer, with a lilac background and glass eyes, three gentlemen peer over in unison. The patent leather bowler hat of the eldest—monocle, tidy goatee, hoary mustache—crowns the pyramid. A bald fellow, puff-cheeked, good-natured, and contrite, lowers his head; beside him the third examiner, who is cut off at his mouth by a green wall—the symmetrical spirals of his pitch black mustache stand out—: sneaky eyes, straight red hair, arched eyebrows.

TOTEM: What should I do to keep it hard while I'm putting it in?

ROSA: Don't think about it.

On the door frame—a bilious and phosphorescent mummy with white eyelids watches us from the shadows—a gypsy woman appears, smoking.

TIGER: What formula should I repeat so as not to be reincarnated as a pig?

Rosa sighs. She takes a tortoise shell case with gold initials out of her purse. With her free hand she destroys an arc of clubs. She opens her vanity case—green glass—she touches up her beauty mark with Chinese ink—that's Rosa for you—she orders a highball with lots of ice . . .

The cobbler's children go without shoes: the decipherer didn't know she wouldn't get to drink it: through the Rembrandt's door, "on tiptoe stealing," the narcotics squad came in.

Turning toward Rosa the crowd held its breath. The five transformers disappeared into the MEN.

The urine vapor: emanation from an offering.

The urinals: oil flasks.

The sink: a fountain of petals.

Sitting on a white china peacock, a yellow god appeared. His middle face was calm; on the lateral ones, protruding fangs,

irritated and globular eyes, noses fuming smoke. The middle
hands together in prayer; the others brandished darts and daggers, bows and arrows.

Five refugee lamas from Nepal emerged sorrow-struck and
devitaminized from the bathroom. The Indian summer was
choking them. They recalled the rancid tea, the reflection of the
copper pitchers in the snow, the barley flour, a wall of white
stones, each inscribed in black with a maxim, the passing of a
yak through the frame of a narrow window, the hand-painted
tankas, once so miraculous, abandoned in the outskirts of Lha-
Ssa.

TUNDRA pointed to the ground.

SCORPION cursed the red demons, instigators of the Chinese
invasion.

With metal helmets imitating heads of owls, of monkey-
eating Philippine eagles, an officer of the peace approached
COBRA:

"Documents . . ."

. . . .

"Drugs . . ."

. . . .

"Dollars . . ."

. . . .

"Detained . . ."

. . . .

He didn't lose a single effect:
he handed him a flower,
a Temple of Eden,

a florin;
he took out his penis and urinated on his feet.

Holding him by the shoulders, the cop cornered him
against the wall.
He buried his claws in his neck.
With his iron beak he perforated his skull.

WHITE

The room is white, the window square.

On the frame of an empty wall—Thought: glowing threads—bordered by lime, compact grey clarity of light rain —forking, interweaving: a fish's flagelli:—a square, now outlined, advances; its edges vibrate.

Further away it flees toward the background, it oscillates —disordered net, disjointed ciphers of fire—a black square is about to fall.

wall
open window rain
far away a closed wicket

:

a white square containing
a grey square containing
a black square.

Two rivers sprout from the penis—your skin is a map:—:
one of them, impetuous, climbs the right side of the body,
hoarse, dragging sand—I cover you with plaster, I draw upon
you with black ink and the finest brush, climbing up the right
side, in a torrent that swells with my breathing, the consonants
mutually entwined;—; the other, tame, clear, goes up the left
side, slow green spirals, algae upon the windings, murmur of
falling pollen, transparency—I draw the vowels upon you.
The center of your body:
six corollas,
six knots,
six couples screwing.

Semen retained:

                 syllables knotting syllables:
                 anklets the ankles,
                 letters the knees,
                 sounds the wrists,
                 mantras the neck.

Semen retained:

                 snake that curls and climbs:
                 rattles among the hinges of
                 vertebrae: around the bones,
                 hoops of scales and glistening
                 skin: oiled cartilage glides,
                 girds the marrow.
                 Lotus that bursts on the top of
                 the skull. Blank thought.

A black line borders the figure
furrowed by three channels
interrupted by flowers

      :

the body
three axes
letters the petals.

They returned to the cellar by way of the port taverns, drinking beer and banging on the show windows—the knitters shrieked—. With the sale of the deceased's jacket they paid for several rounds, a steam bath, tea and marihuana.

They chose two Indonesian girls, newly arrived, who sprayed their beds with jasmine water, masturbated with their fingertips soaked in privet powder, and who attained dilations of the rear thanks to a breathing method of scanning with samsaric sighs.

Pawing and cackling they crossed the rows of Buddhas and other liberated hollow heads. They went down the unfinished steps. They closed the hatchway.

Inside a skull—in the background, in front of a blue oval, a red child, shining and polished, as if made of porphyry, his feet joined at the heels; surrounding him, among purple clouds, the Bodhisattvas—they gathered their victuals, mixed and kneaded them: foul-smelling guts, oozing a black grease from the inner membrane, bristles and eyelids covered by threads of fresh blood, kidneys and testicles, claws, livers. Greenish taint, bile and serum gushed over the bone.

They stripped laughing.
They stuffed themselves with the skull.
They fornicated over nails and blood-clots.

They garnished themselves with gross bone trappings.
With an excess of condiments
and willing brutality
they ate the flesh of men
> of cows
> of elephants
> of horses
> of dogs.

In a tin cup they drank bhang, ground and dissolved in milk and almond juice.
The *five ambrosias* crowned the banquet:

> COBRA's blood
> TIGER's urine
> TUNDRA's excrement
> SCORPION's saliva
> TOTEM's semen.

TO COBRA

Circles (colors), igneous anagrams: you saw the skull upside down, overflowing: the viscera still breathing, the tissues palpitated, rhythmless. Yellow transparency: the humors were ditched in the empty alveoles, gushing over jaw bones, over deeply perforated eye sockets, to the occipital cone, leaving the forehead's fractures exposed, down to the floor, slow clam liquor. Density of pus, hyaline thread of drool, lymph dripping —out of the mouth—of—by the feet—the hanged man, syrup, vein of honey, urine.

From the void sprouted the syllable YAM and from this the blue circle of the air.

RAM red circle

of fire

A   three blinking male heads gave you mocking side glances, opened their mouths, winked, stuck out their tongues at you: giggles, what were they whispering? Their flour-dredged skin was splitting.

Over that tripod, the skull, golden monstrance, *immense like space*.

Over the skull:

OM	white
A	red
HUM	blue

Rays flash from the syllables.

(The potion in the skull boils.)

You laughed to yourself.

"What'd you mix it with?"—the last of the Rembrandt potheads asked you.

The same record. The door that opens. The fluorescent foot.

They were tearing down the bar.

Lie on your right side, your head resting on your open hand. Let your lion's mane fall, vertical to your body fixed in the fury of sleep. On your heart, an octagonal glass. A strong lotus. Colors assigned to each petal. An A on that throne, beast of glistening skin. From another white one, secure, on the top of the head, numerous *a*'s swarm toward the A of the glass: fall of swift signs, minute white birds, milky pebbles, dew returning to the summit.

A red A over your phallus. Burning coals, glare that climbs to the A of the glass, shredded hummingbirds; descent of bleeding arrows.

Swift hoops of frost, garnet atoms circumscribe your body.

When sleep lays siege—mandala of mute animals, slow wave of lava—absorb all the letters into the central letter.

Let the lotus close.

The white wall, the city blurred by rain, the distant wicket.

All the rest and your I: zero.

One dram of bhang drives a wild elephant mad. You knew this when the quiet travelers, cuddled amidst the bar's rubbish, passed you the small black stone. The pachyderm kicks and bellows, the trunk bleeds, he vomits a ton of grass. Ten Pakistani shrimpers hold him down when Ganesa, fuming, reaches the estuary. He sinks into the mud seeking coolness.

With a razor blade you scraped off the texture that was truffled by yellow grains, with your nails you tore off opaque scales. Sweetish papers. You hid them among the loose tobacco.

Nothing.

Yes. The stomach full of ice. Cramps in your feet. A rope that vibrates. A fetid breeze through the nose, quicksilver through the ears. You ran to the MEN. They had torn out the sink.

Dragged iron. The crack of cymbals shaking among flames is followed by that of pomegranates bursting on the ground. Pieces of glass over worn black tiles. Over bare feet, drops of blood. Cobra-stilettos. Perforated tongues.

You were surrounded by the nude possessed, with hooks clamped on their backs and dragging tin shrines, carts gushing honey and puff pastries, hidden by flies, anointed porphyry phalluses.

Families of macaques played piccolos amid trays of figs, flowers, newly-born gods waving rattles, their lips worm-eaten, cankerous giggles.

His straight black hair dropping to his feet over a currant-colored cloak, his forehead smeared with black signs—mice shriek as they devour the wheat—the officiant approached.

Into the fire, burnished with oil, glistening for a moment in the air filled with petals, corpses fell.

Scorpions nested in the ears.

Crows covered the frozen feet.
Mushrooms sprouted on the orbs.
Snakes came into their anuses.

With a teaspoon
they scraped their eyes,
obstinate oysters
gobbled by the monkeys.

Interlocked with one of the Indonesian girls, you were rolling on the ground.

The officiant penetrated the other girl in front of a hundred-handed god with a hundred popped-out pupils, one in each hand.

Along with the smell of his unctuous braided hair, that of burnt viscera also reached you.

INDIAN JOURNAL

I

"Buildings the color of barely dry blood, domes black from the sun, the years, and the rains of the monsoon—others are marble and whiter than jasmine—fantasy-foliaged trees planted in meadows, as geometric as syllogisms, and, within the silence of the pools and of the enamel sky, the shrieks of crows and the silent circles of birds of prey. The rocketing flock of parrots, green stripes that appear and disappear in the quiet air, crosses with the dark grey wings of ceremonious bats. Some return, to go to sleep; others are just waking and fly heavily. It is now almost night and there is still a diffuse light. These tombs are neither of stone nor of gold: they are made of a vegetal and lunar material. Now only the cupolas are visible,

great motionless magnolias. The sky falls into the pool. There is neither down nor up: the world has been concentrated into this serene rectangle. A space into which all fits and which contains only air and a few scattering images."

II

LA BOCA HABLA

La cobra
　　　fabla de la obra
en la boca del abra
　　　　recobra
el habla:
　　　El Vocablo.*

OCTAVIO PAZ.

* *The Mouth Speaks*
The cobra/speaks of the labor/in the mouth of the break/recovers/speech:/ The Vocable. This anagram-poem, which is a play on the word, or vocable, *cobra*, is, evidently, untranslatable. (Translator's Note.)

Among burning timber, the body. Beside the pyre, on the ash-covered ground, a dog licks a bloody white turban and tears it into linen bands. Further away, under an eave, another pile of tree-trunks. Fire technicians hurriedly gather around. A small elephant-god plays among flowers. Copper hand-bells. Death—the pause that refreshes—is part of life.

Carved on the wall, with strong, symmetrical wings, the Mazdean eagles; their prophets' heads crown the doors. Flocks of green parakeets repeat their circles in the sky. Gluttons for eyes, the crows, masters of the dense gardens, keep a watch over the palm-trees.

At dusk, satiated, lethargic, they will relinquish this silence. They will sleep on the barges, upon the red poincianas in the courtyards, amidst humid moldings.

The sentries will pick up the soiled shroud. The skeleton down the well; the bone chips down a drain, to the bay, where nocturnal crustaceans will nibble at them.

I wash. Strokes against the stone. In the small pools, white water. Purple water; the others wring out, lather, rinse, lay them out on the ground. A rancid smell flows from our bodies, steam of sweat and grease that rises to the bridge—the passers-by turn their heads so as not to look at us: one's look can be stained. Hair falls into the ditched lye, feet in the dampness, cracks between the toes.

On the other side of the dunghill, behind the miasma, the train passes.

So much candy
did the elephant-god eat
that his stomach grew big.
From his saddle fell—a mouse.

The moon laughed.
He threw a tusk at her.

I was born. One step. I am dying.

Joining thumb and forefinger in a circle—golden spheres
stuck to their nose, celluloid beauty marks on their cheeks, red
shadow on their eyelids—fifteen hoarse apsarases in battle for-
mation, facing the smoking rooms, jump on those sleepers piled
on the sidewalks, shredding the shirts of passers-by. They're
dancing, that's for sure: on the bodies, the three flexions.

In fluorescent saris, trapped in their superimposed cages,
eating peanuts, the whores shriek. A grimy curtain allows one to
glimpse the bed and the mats from the top of which the family
appraises the panting.

On the window, crack in the glass, a creamy chameleon
sleeps.

Rice on his feet, smeared in red dust, a little monkey-god,
in his concrete temple, entertains the village—his eyes glass
balls, petals stuck to his nose. Startled like storks hearing nocturnal sounds, three heads watch over him upon a neck:
methylene blue, saffron, egg-shell white.

Necklace of flowers, a mustard bull grazes.

A jolting from the turning water wheel. They're singing
—purple turbans in the cloud of dust—; faraway, a monkey's
shriek. They flee: bells on ankles, heavy ear-rings, hoops on
their nostrils. Black signs on their foreheads, the dogs bark
differently.

The branches, fixed. Lianas covered by small purple flies.
Ashen sky. A pheasant.

He quarters a shriveled up chicken smeared with bile, and
bathes it in marmalade; he seasons pieces of raw lamb with

onion, thyme, and mango; while counting the drams he weighs a handful of marihuana, in front of a display shelf of glittering bracelets, he offers a wooden fiddle.

(The wind scatters silk bands—net of gold threads—disperses the cotton piles in flakes, covers the pastry with dust.)

He cures hide, inlays, haggles, resells.

He drinks out of a dark green puddle.

Thermos-bottles of tea, mandarin pull-overs, the monks took over the cave. Yawning, wrapped in blankets, they delivered homage to the Smiling One. The Indians covered up their mouths, laughing behind the columns. Japanese tourists took pictures with a flash.

Frost, invisible crack in the clay: out of the voices, the lowest fell concave in the air; the children's: fragile piccolos, cartilage flageolets, blown tallow lamps.

The walls—scenes from the life of the Diamond—restored the sullied hind-side of the mantras: resin, sweat from the tsampa pit.

Cough. Scratchy throat. Flow of phlegm in the bronchial tubes.

Following the imprints on the floor, worn down by devout feet, the pilgrims wandered around the *dagoba;* they stroked the polished figures with their hands.

Hollow is the urn, a blank white space facing the skeleton, the beggar, the old man; empty is the saddle of the one leaving on a horse, under the fig-tree nobody meditates, the blue-eyed girls in the park, gazelles, listen to nobody.

His arms, swift propellers, shaking the world, a peevish god dances. Beside him—her breasts, half-spheres, her waist, narrow, and wide hips—an undulating goddess in whose arms, perched upon a mouse, an elephant romps—with his twisted bejeweled trunk he caresses her ear. At certain intervals, conch spirals, fossilized sea-horses, grooves from a yellowish rock where a peacock comes to perch, blossom in the carved stone.

In the purple of the cloths, silver lines. The copper dish where stalks burn glitters in the sun. Golden hoop, the light girds the wicker circle of the great bass-drums.

Black faces. The reflection of the flutes undulates; raising their hands, the musicians shake cymbals as though they were branches loaded with fruit. Beneath his aluminum crown, the motionless one looks at his knees; strings of flowers fall down his ears, on both sides of his face, down his arms, to his wrists fastened with trinkets and a watch.

On the ground, the flames slowly consume rice and oil, turrets of red dust, petals. A rancid smell impregnates the air, pink ashes stain the feet.

The tree-trunks, agglutinated roots; destroyed lianas embrace the ruins. The underbrush has invaded the fortresses of the abandoned capital. Birds nest in the brambles that gird the capitals, through the drains of reservoirs black squirrels flee. The monsoon and the drought have cracked the walls buried by dust. Furious monkeys demolish the minarets stone by stone, tearing out cartouches and letters.

Beneath the white dome of a mausoleum, its lantern blinded by the foliage, lime against lime, without stirring its wings, a pheasant moves in uniform circles.

Tied to the end of the baton, a bag of gun powder explodes on the ground: the drum major—a jaundiced, sunken-eyed fellow with polished finger nails—chases the foolish spirits from the streets. Banging great hoarse drums, the retinue arrives at the door not protected by a garland of dry seeds. In the hall, surrounded by a cheering crowd, covered with flowers and flies, the motionless one waits, in a wicker chair. Strings of black blood and a purple drool fall from his lips which the mourners, upon arriving, touch.

THE INDIES[1]

It was covered with trees right down to the river and these were lovely and green and different from ours, and each bore its own fruit or flowers. There were many birds, large and small, which sang sweetly, and there were a great number of palms of a different kind from those of Guinea and from ours. They were of moderate height with no bark at the foot, and the Indians cover their houses with them. The land is very flat.

Their houses were very clean and well swept and their beds and blankets are like cotton nets, and looked like real tents, but without any streets, but rather one here and there, and well swept inside and their adornments very well ordered. All are made of very beautiful palm leaves . . . There were dogs that never barked, and there were nets of palm fiber and lines and horn fish-hooks and bone harpoons and other fishing tackle . . . Trees and fruits of most marvellous flavor . . . Birds and the singing of crickets throughout the night, which everyone enjoyed: the sweet and delicious winds of the entire night, neither hot nor cold . . . Great tree forests, which were very fresh, odorous, by which I have no doubt that there are scent trees in the islands.

All young, as I have said, and all of a good height, a very fine people: their hair is not curly, but straight and as coarse as horse hair, and all have very broad brows and heads, broader than those of any people I have seen before, and their eyes are very fine and not small, and they are not at all black, but the color of Canary Islanders.

A most tame people.

[1] Columbus' Diary.

THE GALLANT INDIES

"Tonight"—the doorman announces—"on this stage, a real god."

The scenery superimposes turrets whose windows—cellophane and wire—are lit from the inside by red lightbulbs; before a leaning tower, the equestrian monument to Queen Victoria.

With a red circle between their eyes, four thick girls are smiling—golden dentures—dancing a Beckoning to Dawn on the proscenium; in the background, on a luminous float which climbs among celluloid clouds, the Sun-God appears with a slicked mustache and golden circles on his cheekbones; at his feet, blinking spotlights of all colors, the throne of the maharajah, his favorite.

The mother of the prince—an exhausted, grey-haired transvestite—rushes around backstage, screaming and fanning herself with a feather fan, followed by a fat woman squeezed into a sari of emeralds and pearls, her nose perforated with tin jewels. The hammering of wooden pegs covers the orchestra's tremolos.

On his golden-pillared bed, under a satin mosquito net, the maharajah sleeps. Shifting shadows behind a screen: a violent mulatto with arched eyebrows, the enemy of the prince and of the Star, approaches. A whirlwind of electric fans ruffles his mane, a red spotlight illuminates him. Raving mad, the Mother appears on a swing, uttering threats and insults.

Rolling of drums. In the background the clouds roll toward the side entrances, revealing a starry sky which suddenly turns red. Clash of cymbals: from the ground, sitting upon a flying ox with bloodshot eyes, waggling his wings and ears, the Sun-God appears. He raises his arm, points to the sky—lights blink—and belts out a war cry that makes the earth quake.

Titans and their mechanical cows push against each other:

each with twelve arms and in their hands, darts and bows, they rush against each other clashing saddles and weapons.

The Malignant One attacks with a spear. Sun responds with a golden saber. Mother hurls a sharp-hooked cockatoo at the Intruder. Like a grasshopper with its own cocoon, the maharajah thumps away against the linen palisade that protects him: the servants, their feet and hands open—as if trying to prove that human extremities are the diagonals of a rectangle—have armored the palisades with swift tapestries around the throne.

The Dark One, like a giant electric fan, makes all his arms rotate—knives in his hands—to grind the Star to pieces. The chopping propeller is already nearing the Luminous One's neck when the latter, pushed by two apsarases who drop from the clouds above, leaps from his chariot, shakes the demon by the nose and throttles his neck. The Villain pops out his eyes, sticks out a plushy yellow tongue, kicks madly . . . and falls to the ground amidst brimstone flames, broken knives and un-screwed ears which leap toward the audience where the fanatics grab for them.

Indigo, saffron, white: silk strips over the ground; against the stone steps that go down to the river, the washerwomen slap their saris. Cow heads emerge from the water: on the tips of their horns, silver cones.

On the opposite shore, under a cliff and of the same yellow ochre, a village of huts with flattened dirt floors. From above, the monkeys, who plundered the forest, climb down clinging to the rocks with their nails, hungry for oranges. Entrenched on the roofs, they assail the pilgrims arriving in carts.

To keep the fat demons from entering, a pillar obstructs the temple door. Next to his copper pitcher, an ashen man, covered by his own scorched hair, strings a liana with red-lettered palm tablets.

Under the figs, old women weave. Into the dark green water of the pond, boys dive from the crown of a niche where a god, with half a mustache and one breast, receives purple flowers. The travelers, bare-chested, wash the bands of their white turbans.

In the cell's shadows, oil lamps sway. Caressed slowly with ointments, covered with fresh flowers, the basalt phallus shines in the center: a ciphered line marks the frenum. The thick cream with which the officiant bathes it remains on the polished plate that serves as its base.

Behind the reverberation of the dense air, Brahmans burn their offerings; in front, blurred by the smoke and standing beside a gate, others absent-mindedly intone the ritual words and give water to the devotees—who bring milky annona pyramids, split coconuts, small bananas, coins and petals—for them to drink and anoint their heads.

The forefinger anointed with oil, with red dust, swiftly traces the sign on the forehead.

Concentric imprints hollow out the descending floor, tilted like a roof. Upside down, fixed in their rolling toward the stream, the bases of the columns have remained among lifted slabs: the air is chipping sand off their edges. Superimposed strata of different veins shape the ruins: horizontal lines, parallel like the marks left on a wall by the flood.

Temple after temple—birds fly straight through them— corroded, lean.

From the niches where lizards nest, armless, marble children watch us, their eyes circled by golden lines. In a puddle of urine, alone in a cell, a lunatic repeats the twenty-four names.

Fig-trees on the frontispieces. Between the branches of a dry ashen tree, the moon.

The straight middle line, pure lime: the lateral curves, bloody: the trident marks the figures of the heaped gods, the stones on the wall surrounding the pool, the forehead of the great elephant that the Brahmans bathe and perfume all day long.

On the ground, after the ceremonies, crushed flowers, yellow rice, incense, walnuts, shit have remained. Only once a year does the sun light up the entire mustard mast.

Great plaster monkeys, peacocks with inlaid stones, three-headed gods and a golden-winged ox—the feathers chiseled like a bird's—all await the day of the feast, crammed into a stinking corridor.

Upon the pyramids of figures screwing, the Brahmans flourish brushstrokes of hot pink, pastel blue, canary yellow.

The mirroring of the fish-filled rectangle, untouched for millennia.

A naked boy, his skin impregnated with ashes and ciphered with red signs, sounding a receptacle of coins, crosses the street.

His bare feet, embroidered; his worm-eaten feet, golden threads; his hair, anointed with coconut oil.

Beside the sea, in the lower chamber you sleep, on your couch of cobras.

Sleeping among sacks one on top of the other, in a steam of rotten grapes, of milk, of excrement and vomit, playing, rolled inside burrows of hay, fornicating, waiting on the platform invaded in the morning by a coppery vapor, of burnt rubber, opening their mouth, digging in the garbage, walking.

Wrapped in white sheets, taking shelter from the rain,

under the portals, upon the sidewalks covered with glass where the harbor birds, choking from the black air. DRINK KALI-COLA, come to fall.

Twisted tin statues support the domes stained by the clapping of crows' wings. In wax, the equestrian effigy of the donors fixed in a funereal smile. Big mother-of-pearl flowers: petals spill strings of water. Behind enameled gates, semi-nude officiants in the night await. Green mosaic fountains; around them, aluminum Venuses offer apples; amid glass peacocks, luminous, blue-eyed prophets with slicked mustaches examine marble books. Columns decorated with minute mirrors reflect the light of the morning sun.

Upon a wide pearl throne, a boy with a shaved skull smiles; his legs folded, the soles of his feet turned upwards, his enormous eyes bordered by black lines, on his forehead a bluish diamond.

Through the ambulatory—gallery of mirrors—the officiants approach, balancing on their hands pyramids of copper dishes pierced through by a rod.

Nothing that grows on the ground. Nothing that contains blood. Nose and mouth covered by a thick cloth.

The floor is majolica: wild bellflowers, glazed fruits, butterflies. In order to worship the Whitest One, we rest our bare feet on the tiles' central rosettes where the reflections from stained-glass windows—red blots—vibrate. Hundreds of garlands surround him, birds that fly away when we open the door to the sanctuary, escaping toward the glare of the central courtyard where naked bricklayers white-wash arches that are crowned by needles, weather-cocks, golden bulbs.

Throughout the rainbow-saturated sky, upon embroidered barges—the prows are heads of animals, the sails, parasols—the worshipers spill petals over Mahavira, crown of a human pyramid lifted by twenty-four identical ascetics. With four arms

in a swastika and on her shoulder a sitar, an ostrich-riding goddess follows them—a string of pearls in the bird's beak—;
another goddess, upon a cockatoo with blazing feet, brandishes
darts and pronged wheels with her eight arms.

Further away, two princes wearing Persian turbans, standing over the knot formed by their eel tails, cool the prophet with
white fans. From the throne emerges a luminous ribbon which,
undulating like the tail of a kite, climbs to the sky where its
course repeats a caravan's: rounding the mountain, with har-
nessed elephants and banners, with a thousand trumpets and
monkeys, King Shrenik approaches the alabaster domes.

In the cracks of the flagstone pavement, curly hair; red
curds, like sealing wax. A smell of lukewarm viscera, blood clots
and flowers impregnates the air: to placate her anger, to make
her forget us, we offered sacrifices to the Terrible One.

Cries. Someone is blowing a conch shell. Your face is black,
bloody are your fangs, your necklace is strung with skulls, your
feet are cooled in the splatterings of slashed jugulars.

The city cracks under the shelter of your cloak. The salty
wind corrodes stones and men.

In bamboo stretchers they carry them: their glassy eyes
open, their foreheads tarnished, on their lips two white butterflies.

The soaked shroud; a vermilion dust, grain thrown in the
air, the stain.

The hum of bazaars around the temple. On the walls red
blemishes. Scribbled figures; sanskrit signs written with coal.
The glare from the factories brightens the muddy river water,
the iron bridge.

*Death is neither here nor there. She's always beside us,
industrious, infinitesimal.*

The elephants clasp trunks to greet each other imitating the handshake of men.

Bearded man with oval eyes; you, naked woman, are dancing to the rhythm of a triangle, with your arms arched you display an apple in front of your forehead.

Standing, naked, you write me a letter.

With a burnt wooden stick you stretch the corner of your eyelids, you lean your elbow upon the head of a servant.

You forget the thorn; you look at yourself in a circle of polished metal.

A monkey licks you.

A scorpion undresses you.

Two crowned *nagas* intertwine their tails: scaly braid. One of them displays a bottle of perfume.

I with woman's hair, you, in front, bent over, the palms of your hands on the floor. My fingers leave imprints on your waist, where strings of pearls are knotted, your buttocks and breasts girded.

With his turban on, a whiskered warrior, laughing with his mouth wide open, penetrates a mare with a member as wide as a horse's; his companion, mounted on a bench, mockingly covers his face; another drinks wine from a conch-shell.

Head against the floor, feet up, each of my arms clasped by the legs of a naked woman: my ringed fingers penetrate them.

Seen from behind—her hairdo: a tower of jewels—a third one comes to sit between my thighs. I force her. Smiling, my sentries make her sink down. To let it further in, you bend your legs, raise your feet off the ground. Tiny servants come to help you and get sucked by maids who, at the same time, play with little monkeys.

Beside the river, to a cabin, you pulled me along by the tunic. With an andante step you glided through the rushes.

Thin like a lioness's, your waist reminded me of the frame of a *dombori* drum. You arched your back. The bees buzzed in shiny circles around the lotus of your feet.

Your breasts are full spheres which my fingers stroke, a golden point on the corners lengthens your eyes, your straight nose, your eyebrows sketched in a single stroke. You carry a cymbal, I a flower.

So numerous and pretty are your ornaments that it seems as if a hundred thousand golden bees have lighted on your body, the music of hoops that repeat the fifth note of the scale on your ankles is as sweet as honey.

Dyed with lacquer, your big toes glitter in the sun.

I spent the whole night sipping a little gazelle, in whose eyes there was such a delicious languor that I could not go to sleep.

The guru sprinkles his face with flour, lights up his chilom, mumbles a salute to the pink apsarases of dawn; in the kitchen, behind a red steam of boiling pimientos, the disciples fondle a glass statue; like the master, obese, its hair in a bun.

Parasols of woven palm leaves, marked in red with Bengali writing, shade the lethargic ones. As the fog lifts, the praying men go down the steps, with copper pitchers.

Before a multi-armed celluloid doll in a dress of pink and purple satin, the chorus of faithfuls takes turns around the microphone so that the music doesn't stop; they've hung speakers on the poles so that people can hear it way on the other shore. A scarlet cloud, flowing from a blazing hill, perfumes the goddess; a frog-like dwarf moans at her feet.

Brahmans smear the temple columns with sealing wax; monkeys, hanging by their tails, swing on the bell clappers. Three immersions. Three times I drink water from my hands, which in silence I return to the river. A red disk burns the empty, sandy plain on the other side, and lights the motionless barges, the offerings—wicker trays dragged by the current—a circle of ashes which the dogs sniff.

Wooden balconies. Film posters carpet the façades. Gold sheath: the Nepalese towers of a temple. Two yellow tigers stand guard in front of the house of the man who collects the cremation taxes.

With a vanity case and a small stick he covers his body, already whitened, with what he copies out of a book: with sandalwood dust a yellow rectangle on his forehead, a red V on his arm, tridents on the hands, on a cinnabar background the repeated name on the sole of his foot. Shabby chamber maids bring him fresh flowers, sponge cake, a few coins; they sweep the floor-boards, spruce up the fringes of the parasols. Two little boys show him, inside small earthenware vessels, lighted candles which they then place on the bank and push away with their hands like paper boats. He streaks his genitals in green, a silver ring circles his foreskin.

Brahmans will spray his shroud: stuck to the cachetic body, soaked drapery. They will roll him from the canvas stretcher onto trunks of wood. With a torch, through the mouth, his relatives will set him on fire. *You will leave Varanasi, but Varanasi will not easily leave you. Something somewhere inside you will not ever be the same again.*

The flood that draws near, dragging the sand on the bottom, will carry us to the delta, to the sea.

Beside potbellied dwarf-Vishnu, the worshiper—a key hangs from a white string crossing his chest—intones the prayer. He hums, murmurs, whispers names—the light through the branches lengthens the shadow of his body on the wall—; with his forefinger he touches the engraved letters.

In front of the temple, on the reverberating plain, two

yoked oxen revolve around a well. An adolescent in a white turban drives and whips them. Earthenware jars draw the water and
pour it into a gully; the ribbon follows the furrows, the edges of
the village, the path which undulates through different greens,
to the pools of the temple, where a blackish canal, amid cobra
snares, pours out the milk of the offerings.

In the horizon, blurred, four minarets stand guard over the
white mausoleum. Closer, among small handfuls of gold, a
farmer pushes his plow; down the road go the muleteers, their
reflections in a river framed by the dark arabesques of the
Fortress.

Through the white latticework, the texture of stars piercing
marble walls, white saris float in the wind; through perforated
polygons—meeting of clear dots—turbans. The brick façade
decomposes—minute red stains—seems to evaporate. Through
empty light-shafts the sun penetrates to the lower chamber: a
thick cloth, of black felt, conceals the Prophet's tomb; a repeated phrase glitters on the threshold.

Pigeons take flight in unison, as if they had heard a shot,
and circle over the immense courtyard; they return to perch on
the fountain, on the parallel mats where barefoot devotees
kneel, and touch the ground with their foreheads. Beside a mimbar, an old man in a white beard and black turban balances his
concave hands together, as if they contained a thick fluid, ready
to filter between his fingers; another spells out a scroll with
worn edges.

Outside, at the foot of the mosque, peddler stands, statue
bazaars are crowded together; dealers auction off miniatures,
tankas painted over with the wrong gods, coarse ivory deities,
torn Tibetan banners. An enormous orange sun sinks between
the minarets, in a spotted sky; the beckoning voice of the muez-
zin silences the hammering of the blacksmith shops, the shouts
of the laundrymen, the tinkling of copper-filled tents. The ring-

ing of bicycles and car horns mingles with radios' high, syrupy soprano voices, xylophones and harps. Rusty auto bodies, broken engines, tires are all piled to the porticos; rancid motor oil gushes from zinc; a pungent stench rises out of the scrap iron labyrinth.

The pigeons take flight again, extending their course to the bridge, to the brick fort from whose balconies, fringed by dark arabesques, one can see in the distance, where the furrows meet, the white mausoleum, and trembling as though behind a river of alcohol, the four minarets, the golden crescent.

The children stroll hand-in-hand through the garden centered around the tombs of princes; they climb up to the empty niches, remain embraced in silence, reading; they clamber to the terraces, race down, climb again, sing. One is biting into sugar cane, another throws oranges. They carry coloring books, chalk, cups, and little green plastic canteens.

Dry pools break up the lawn. Streaked with chisels, the vaults bear English nicknames, figures, dates which from afar are white erasures. Splinters of the rim on the pediment.

Climbing stairways that lead nowhere, sloping walls, empty hemispheres. As they pass along numbered edges, shadows reproduce the Earth's curvature, cipher the stars' altitude, postulate a fixed Sun. On the stairs erased by the rain, each afternoon reconfirms these measurements. Bronze astrolabes have remained among the ruins, discarded, broken.

The exact time.

In your couch of intertwining cobras, upon an ocean of milk, you sleep, naked. A thousand scaly heads crown your head. You breathe slowly. Your body gives in to the soft rings; upon your open hands, the emblems rest.

Perhaps you are listening to the immense banyan trees that

border the pool; the wind and the birds shake their thick black threads.

Through a covered bridge, the devotees come to anoint your feet, they drink from the orange water ditched between your legs, they touch the knots of the tails. Petals and *paisas* cover you; beside your head smeared with yellow dust, a copper jar shines.

From the far south pilgrims have come to sing to you. Two stone pigs stand guard beside the bell they ring in your honor.

Perpetual propellers, your arms have chopped up everything. Among the unwinding and flame-spitting cobras, your body has revolved. Serene, smiling, your gestures underlined by circles of fire disrupted by your own flight, assembled once more, swift, glowing borders of fine threads, lightning flashes of slow rainbows. A solar crown follows your body's undulations and repeats them in the space that curves around your arms, when they spin.

Your destructive dance has extinguished the Earth. Now, panting, you contemplate the devastated space. Your eyelids are heavy. Your arms and legs give in to the tranquil reptiles. You rest your head. One by one your muscles relax. Your eyes half-opened, you see the winter sky. The night wind effaces the trees.

From your navel the lotus flower will emerge, and from her, the creator.

You will dance again.

Go back to sleep.

Behind the beet baskets, the rice heaps, the tarnished glass-case, in the warehouse mist, merchants weigh the tea. Painted on the door, among parrots devouring flowers, the seven Bodhisattvas. Through the glass, beyond the roofs, and the carved beams, the EYES of a golden tower, the mountain.

They pass by on bicycles, thick bells sound upon the angles of pagodas, they touch their foreheads. The supports of the eaves are yellow goats with enormous phalluses. On the steps, vendors lay out tablets strung with red letters, in Pali, Sanskrit calendars, Nepalese berets, mandalas, maps.

To the goddess spearing a buffalo, we offer small bananas; over the blood-drooling skulls held in her multiple hands, we scatter petals; raw rice on the ground, which avid pigeons devour. With a harmonica, a fiddle and a triangle—a little boy sings—the old men of the neighborhood, sitting on a mat, regale the entrance; in the courtyard, candles light up a cup filled with flowers, a wheel, a swastika: among gold flags fouled by birds Buddha teaches. Mantra banners. The Liberated is surrounded by an eagle-god of shining metal, a Mongolian-eyed marshal who unfolds a scroll and two lions with red pupils.

Beneath conical roofs, demons open women by their legs, quartering them. So that the faithful can draw the prescribed signs on their foreheads we have installed small mirrors on all the walls.

A metal ribbon falls from the top of the pagoda, through the superimposed roofs, down to the lowest, which it touches.

Among the sculptures in the courtyard, sacred lambs are fornicating in a flock.

Smell of hashish and sandalwood.

Over a row of prayer wheels which spin with a metallic murmur—pilgrims are pushing them: the formulas unfold in the wind—in niches with broken doors, the Enlightened receive at their feet children who play; monkeys come to steal the offerings and greedily devour their clothes, then they clamber on top of the great golden scepter—one of them sucks an egg—they jump down to the white lump of the stupa, whose cement is stained by drippings, from the peak, of the yellow left by the rain; from there they contemplate the thirteen heavens—one by one—the crest, surrounded by lamps, ending in a lightning rod.

Upon shabby, parallel carpets, the pupils are reciting mantras. Surrounding Siddhartha, a thousand silvery statues; facing the shelf that contains them, atop a tall arm-chair, a lama wearing glasses and a red hat conducts the prayer. Piled on the seats, model temples of marzipan, yellowish cloaks, goblets of tsampa tea. An acolyte bangs the circular drum hanging at the entrance, another puffs his cheeks, turns red, manages to blow a horn and then a conch shell; a third one, under his cloak, opens a box of Ovaltine. They whisper, fling paper balls and planes, make signs and faces at each other, flawlessly repeating the Mani. One stands up, from the shelf takes a water flask and some pastries, opening a grimy awning he throws them into the courtyard; another falls asleep, bangs another with his head, urinates on his own cloak; his partner tickles his ears.

From the top of the hill we hear the stampede of cymbals, the only note from the great folding horns which the monks transport on skates, their voices, continuous and hoarse.

On the ceiling centered by a glass globe with a model plane from the Royal Nepal Airlines, the Great Mandala of the Irritated and Knowledge-Hoarding Deities; the walls are scenes from the life of the Diamond. A little bird comes to bathe in one of the offering chalices. The fresh air penetrates the windows sealed by metallic screens. With some effort a peasant spins a prayer wheel of his own size.

From the tower of the great stupa, the eyes of the Pious watch us—blue-dyed eyebrows, enameled eyelids; a red hoop girds the pupils. On the summit, colored banners flash in all directions from the golden parasol; the printed prayers float in the wind.

"Here I am, kids, that is to say your Grand Lama, and therefore chief of the world famous stupa that we have before us. Yes, white shaggy monks, I am fulfilling my karma in this

suburban hovel, selling the ancient tankas of the Order and trafficking in copper scepters, now rusted green, in order to support
the last lamas of the Yellow Hat.

"With the tablets of the Canon, the portable instruments, a
herd of yaks, a few ritual masks that we were able to collect in
the haste of our departure and a collection of dies for printing
banners, the Congregation, watched over by the Ancestors,
crossed the coldest valleys, the highest mountains in the world.
One of the dignitaries who precedes me was forced to emigrate;
they display the other at the popular courts in those provinces of
Outer Mongolia, so northerly and snowy that not even storks
reach there in the summer."

TUNDRA: What should I do in order to convert to Bud-
dhism?

THE GRAND LAMA: Shave your head. Ah, and please, if
you really want to get into the "mainstream," stop all violence
right now. The French ambassador came to see me this morning;
in the afternoon his son killed a tiger in Rajahstan. From here
they went to the Ashoka Club and drank rice beer. Verily I say
unto you, kids of Holland, that it is Thirst that prevents you
from seeing the un-composed, the un-created, that which is
neither permanent nor ephemeral. What do you think of this
ancient painting, a gift from an incarnate lama in Bhutan?

SCORPION: I'm afraid of dying in an accident, what should
I do?

DESIRED ANSWER: The aggregates that compose men, oh
pale ones, are nothing but products lacking the least reality: to
understand this produces a joy that ignores death.

REAL(ity's) ANSWER: Come on, man! That's what amulets
are for! This one, for example—he takes from a table a dagger
with four blades and emblems on the handle—sought-after by
several western museums, envelops the body of its owner in an

invulnerable halo. Or this one—he shakes a parchment rattle, two pellets beat it, on the end of a thread—which surely you have never seen: it protects and fortifies.

TOTEM: How can one eliminate anguish?

THE GRAND LAMA: Sit with your legs crossed—and, dropping his slippers, he crosses his own, which are squeezed into yellow suede pants—your back straight, your attention alerted. A circle. Inscribe a square inside it. In the center, a favorite deity of yours. Concentrate on it. Naturally, in order to start, a support is necessary, a painted mandala, like this one—and he evolves, over the carpet, a painted cloth with concentric geometries—so miraculous and ancient that for you, for such a noble task, I would give it up for a few dollars: rupees of this country could not come near it, and, of course, much less those of India.

TIGER: Which is the true road to Liberation?
THE GRAND LAMA remains silent. A silly giggle (in the next room, on a sofa, his children talk over a red telephone, made of plastic).

The smell of burnt sheets, the steam rising from the banks of the river: slowly, we breathe.

For three days we shall sleep under the eaves, beside the small tile platforms, looking at the water. We shall give alms to the crippled who crawl around with tin cans. On the fourth night we shall return home.

Inside a windowless dump—the sweetish smell of adjacent pyres and of curry stagnated—sitting near the frying pans, on the dirt floor, the yogis who have gone up north for today's celebration are reciting the morning precepts, and frying vegetables. With ashes from the coal stoves they smear their bodies; carefully they smooth out their hair, anointed with juniper oil. They allow people to look at them, but not with glasses.

The pilgrims scream at the temple doors, crowd along the river, break through the lines of soldiers and run toward the courtyard in order to touch the great golden Nandin—flowers on his claws, on his knees three white stripes. A silver trident and a tambourine stand out between the roofs.

As the sun climbs between the swollen trunks and the light filters through treetops, in the small corroded temples phalluses start appearing, in rows. The women who perfume them, the vermilion and gold of their dresses, interrupt at times, for an instant, the perfect succession of cylinders.

Monkeys steal and shred the clothes which the devotees have left on the shore. At the sound of three grimy musicians, a chubby little girl dances; her brother tells, in English, the story of the guru who blinded a hippie with a stone, he imitates the drowning of the holy man who, because of his wine-drinking, rolled into the river.

A Sherpian peasant displays in a basin the movement of a few river snails, and on a scale, handfuls of marihuana which four long-haired boys bargain for, in Dutch.

The women let the shiny bands of their saris float; the shadows of partridges crossing from one shore to the other are black arrows upon the stony bottom floor.

Stained by the cremation ashes, by the grime of the bath, and of spit, the thread of water follows its course down the valley, snaking between the rocks, sinking into the flats, digging a ravine in whose walls, sheltered in the crevices, the friends of the birds meditate, mutely.

Then it descends to the royal baths—two cobras feed the pond.

On the signboards, the first ideograms; on both sides of the road, successive terraces down to the dry stream—strips of shiny sand—like a swelling wave.

The farmers come down from the huts in single file, under the row of red trees; the wicker cabins are clear dots on the ochre slope. The morning wind unfolds the smoke from the pottery workshops into hazy layers. On the hills white banners float over piles of stones covered with black writing.

Where the road ends, on the other side of the bridge, the abrupt cliff of the mountains; frozen threads come down from the top.

A cement elephant, upon which a boy rides, hoisting a book, precedes the solid, parallel constructions covered by the black monograms of the March. Further up, between the peaks, maybe the wind will make the prayer wheels spin, aligned upon the walls of the abandoned monasteries, upon the altars buried by the snow.

The red-cloaked monks recite a greeting to Avalokitesvara. From left to right they follow with their forefingers the letters inscribed on the white tablets which they hold up to the outside and protect from the sun with a cloth.

A neon tube lights golden Gautama whose lips are stretched in a rictus. Silk banners embroidered with colors today carpet the columns and the roof. Beside dishes of pastries, pots of smoking tea, rattles and candies, the children hang white tulle bands from the garland that frames a giant poster, in acrylic colors, of a young haloed lama, and from vases decorated by myopic and prognathic kings, in profile.

At dawn we shall start out again, until upon the horizon, the peaceful and twilight-hoarding deities show their orange fingers. Then we shall contemplate silently the slowness of the sun sinking between the snowy valleys, on the other side of the mountains, beside the great and now empty stupas and the EYES clouded over the towers of the native land.

In the echo left by a cymbal, the deepest of the four voices will pronounce the syllables:

May the lotus flower
be, by the Diamond, joined.